# My Life as a Youtuber

## Praise for **My Life as a Book:**

* "Janet Tashjian, known for her young adult novels, offers a novel that's part *Diary of a Wimpy Kid*, part intriguing mystery.... Give this to kids who think they don't like reading. It might change their minds."
—*Booklist*, starred review

## Praise for **My Life as a Stuntboy:**

"Fans of the first will be utterly delighted by this sequel and anxious to see what Derek will turn up as next."
—*The Bulletin*

## Praise for **My Life as a Cartoonist:**

"This entertaining read leaves some provoking questions unanswered—usefully."
—*Kirkus Reviews*

## Praise for **My Life as a Joke:**

"At times laugh-out-loud funny ... its solid lesson, wrapped in high jinks, gives kids something to think about while they giggle."
—*Booklist*

## Praise for **My Life as a Gamer:**

"What did I think? I thought the book was wonderful."
—Kam (from Goodreads)

## Praise for **My Life as a Ninja:**

"Oh My God this book was so amazing!!!!!!!!!!"
—Caleb (from Goodreads)

JANET TASHJIAN

with cartoons by
JAKE TASHJIAN

Christy Ottaviano Books
Henry Holt and Company
New York

Henry Holt and Company, *Publishers since 1866*
175 Fifth Avenue, New York, NY 10010
mackids.com

Henry Holt® is a registered trademark of Macmillan
Publishing Group, LLC

This book is an independent work of fiction and is not
authorized, endorsed, or sponsored by Google, Inc. (owner
of YouTube).

Our books may be purchased in bulk for promotional,
educational, or business use. Please contact your local
bookseller or the Macmillan Corporate and Premium Sales
Department at (800) 221-7945 ext. 5442 or by e-mail at
MacmillanSpecialMarkets@macmillan.com.

Library of Congress Control Number: 2017945044

ISBN 978-1-62779-892-1

First edition, 2018 / Designed by Patrick Collins

Printed in the United States of America by
LSC Communications, Harrisonburg, Virginia

10  9  8  7  6  5  4  3  2  1

For Jessica Rose Felix

# BEST CLASS EVER

History. Language arts. Geography.
Science.

To succeed in any of them, you
have to be a pretty good reader—
which unfortunately I'm not.

But our school is offering a new
after-school elective this winter that
doesn't require ANY reading. Plus, the
subject is one of my absolute favorite
things in the world.

elective

lottery

contain

YouTube!

Because every kid in school wanted to sign up, Mr. Demetri decided to have a lottery. I've never won a raffle in my life, so I was shocked when Ms. McCoddle posted the lucky few students who made the cut and Matt and I were on the list!

Umberto and Carly were on the waiting list—as if anyone's going to drop out of such an awesome elective. And when we find out the teacher is Tom Ennis—a local stand-up comic with his own popular YouTube channel—Matt and I can't contain our excitement. We race down the hallway screaming until Mr. Demetri tells us to knock it off.

"Tom Ennis is HILARIOUS," I tell Matt on our way to the cafeteria. "We're going to have a blast."

Our new teacher's YouTube channel is called LOL Illusions. He's gotten hundreds of thousands of subscribers by being a digital magician like Zach King. Every week he uploads a new video featuring an unbelievable trick. He's not a magician in the traditional sense; instead he's a wizard in post-production who edits his clips with special effects to make them look like magic.

In the 240 videos he's uploaded, he's turned a photo of a kitten into a real kitten in the palm of his hand, he's leaped into a speeding convertible without ever opening the door, he's jumped on his bed so hard he falls through and lands underneath it, and he's thrown a guitar into the dryer and shrank it into an ukulele.

Tom's buddy Chris is usually in

ukulele

the background too, texting on his phone and ignoring Tom as he pulls off these outrageous stunts. The joke is Chris never looks up quick enough to take a picture of the stunt and misses the magic trick every time. It's one of my favorite channels, one that I subscribed to immediately after watching Tom's first clip, where he "makes" dinner by reaching into a cookbook and pulling out a whole turkey.

"Stop rubbing it in," Umberto finally tells us. "I'd give anything to be in that class."

If I added up all the hours Matt, Carly, Umberto, and I have spent watching YouTube, the number would be bigger than all the hours we've logged at school since kindergarten, combined. (The total would be even larger if they'd let us use our phones during class.) But looking at YouTube from the point of view of a CREATOR versus a VIEWER is gigantic. The class starts tomorrow and I already know I'll be up all night, too excited to sleep.

gigantic

casserole

When I get home, Mom's in the kitchen putting a casserole in the oven. She must not have a full schedule at her veterinary practice today, because she's in her running clothes instead of her usual scrubs, which means she just got off her treadmill. I try to peek into the oven to see how many vegetables she's hiding in the casserole, but she closes the oven door and asks about my first day back at school after the holiday break.

I blurt out the news about the

ruckus

prehistoric

YouTube class with so much volume that Dad hurries downstairs.

"What's the ruckus?" he asks. "Are they giving out free puppies at school?"

"Even better." I repeat the story about my new class.

I'm not sure if it's to help celebrate or to show how cool he is, but Dad pulls his phone from his pocket and opens up his YouTube app. "This might be the funniest thing I've ever seen." He holds up the screen and plays a video of David coming back from the dentist. My father's laughing so hard I don't have the heart to tell him how prehistoric that clip is.

It's always hard to concentrate on my homework, but tonight it's especially difficult. Bodi curls underneath the kitchen table as I work, content to just sleep by my feet. Our capuchin, Frank, on the other hand, is jumping around so much, I begin to wonder if he can reach the coffee-pot from his crate.

We've been a foster family for Frank for almost two years, letting him acclimate to humans before going on to monkey college in Boston where he'll learn to help people with disabilities. Every time I think of Frank having to leave, I work myself into such a frenzy that one of my parents has to calm me down. Tonight I'm ALREADY in a frenzy, just thinking about how lucky I am to take part in tomorrow's elective.

YouTube, here I come!

acclimate

# OUR VERY OWN
# COMEDY NERD

When Mr. Owens monitored our comedy club elective last year, we looked at him as a necessary evil. With Tom Ennis, however, it's like having a rock star for a teacher. When the final bell rings, every other kid races out of school. But all twelve of us lucky students hurry into another classroom, eager to get started. Tom strolls in ten minutes

strolls

after school ends, wearing a GoPro camera with an elastic band around his head.

"Hey, kids, I hope you don't mind if I film our sessions."

Not only is he going to teach us—he's going to make us stars! We all sit a little taller in our seats, waiting for our close-ups.

"First of all," he begins, "I'm Tom. But Mr. Demitri INSISTS you guys call me Mr. Ennis, so we'll have to go with that."

He's wearing the skinniest jeans I've ever seen with a beat-up pair of Chuck Taylors. His hair is to his shoulders, with half of it pulled back in a small bun, held up by the band of his camera. His T-shirt is faded and says HAIRY MASTODON, which I'm guessing is a band. Given how

mastodon

larger-than-life he looks in his videos, I can't believe how normal he seems in person.

Mr. Ennis hands out sheets of paper for us to distribute. "These are release forms. If you don't sign them, you can't take the class."

distribute

I'm not sure what a release form is but I've watched enough TV to know you're not supposed to sign anything without reading it first. It hardly matters because there's no way I'm NOT taking this class. But leave it to Maria to raise her hand and ask Mr. Ennis to explain.

permission

"Signing a release means you give me permission to use video footage of you however I please," he answers.

Of COURSE I'm taking this class, but now I'm as confused as Maria is.

"So if I sign this," I ask, "you can take the footage you're shooting now, add a few filters, and turn me into an orangutan with bananas sticking out of my ears?"

orangutan

"If I want to, yes." Mr. Ennis takes out his cell and rapidly starts typing. "I'm writing that down. I love orangutans."

Matt turns and gives me a thumbs-up like I'm the class genius but I'm just secretly hoping our new teacher doesn't turn me into a cyber-primate for his own amusement.

primate

Mr. Ennis doesn't write on the whiteboard like a normal teacher. He's sitting cross-legged on the desk to face us instead. "The first thing you need to know about being a youtuber is that it's a full-time job,

cross-legged

even when it's a part-time job. There are a million clips uploaded *every single minute of every single day,* and if you want your show to stand out, you need to be thinking about your show 24/7." He looks at us and grins. "So ... you think you're up for it?"

The answer from the class is a resounding YES.

"Good." He pulls a stick of gum out of his pocket. I get excited to see what kind of trick he might do with it, but he just shoves it into his mouth. It's still cool, and in all my years of school, I can't recall ever seeing a teacher chew gum in class.

recall

As Mr. Ennis continues to talk about "creative content," I catch myself focusing more on his headcam than his words. If Ms. McCoddle or any of my other teachers wore one of these, I'd be more distracted than usual and would NEVER retain anything they said.

We spend the rest of the class watching online videos, which is AMAZING. Mr. Ennis said he had to run clips by Mr. Demetri first to make sure they were appropriate to show in school so of course we beg him to show us the ones that Demetri didn't allow. I can tell that Mr. Ennis WANTS to show us but also wants to keep his job. Instead, he shows us a video of a girl instructing viewers how to blow-dry their hair like a movie star while her little brother pretends to be a zombie attacking her from behind.

instructing

"That's the mystery," he says. "Does the girl not know her brother's making fun of her or is she in on the joke and asked him to do it? There's no way for us to know—and that's half the fun."

I slowly turn to Matt, who's grinning as mischievously as I am. Neither of us needs to speak because we're both thinking the same thing:

We're starting our own YouTube channel!

# EUREKA!

Even before Mr. Ennis's class, I was incubating ideas for a YouTube show.

incubating

"Don't get me wrong," Matt says as we grab a table in the cafeteria a few days later. "It sounds great, but having our own show is probably a ton of work."

"A lot of fun too. I'm with Derek on this." Umberto reaches across the table and gives me a fist bump.

practical

tutorial

macaroons

As usual, Carly is the most practical of the four of us. "I'm sure your teacher could point us to a good online tutorial. I think the four of us could create a GREAT YouTube channel." She offers us some macaroons from her bag. (Carly thankfully always brings enough dessert for all of us.)

I hate to bring up a sore spot while we're eating her food, but I ask Carly how the four of us are going to create a YouTube channel when Matt and I are the only ones taking the class.

She seems surprised; Umberto does too. "I just assumed since you guys were lucky enough to get in that you'd share the information with us."

Umberto then nods, looking as

expectant as Carly is. I turn to Matt, who plays with the cookie crumbs instead of helping me out.

expectant

"Of course we will," I finally answer. I reach for another cookie and wait for the awkward moment to pass. Matt finally jumps in.

"We could do a Let's Play channel," he says. "If that's not too complicated."

"You forget I've been taking computer classes for years," Umberto says. "I know how to do all KINDS of things, including an LP channel."

And just like that, lunchtime turns into a production meeting. Matt still thinks we should do a video game walk-through show, Umberto wants us to do challenges like eating handfuls of ground cinnamon until we choke (uh, no thanks), and Carly

cinnamon

possibilities

stipulation

snowboarding

thinks we should do epic sports fails. By the time lunch is over, we've come up with twenty-two possibilities for our new channel.

"There's one stipulation," Umberto tells Matt and me on our way to class. "You guys have GOT to stop talking about Mr. Ennis."

Umberto's right—Matt and I haven't shut up about our new teacher. We can't help it—we're on fire with new ideas.

Back in class, I'm a little freaked out by Ms. McCoddle's sunburn. I guess she went snowboarding at Big Bear this weekend so her face is red but the area around her eyes is white from wearing goggles. She keeps taking lotion from her purse to apply to her skin. Just looking at her makes me itchy.

When Matt and I had Ms.

McCoddle in kindergarten, we'd spend the first hour talking about what we did the night before. Now we barely sit down before Ms. McCoddle tells us to open our history books. "Today we begin the Industrial Revolution," Ms. McCoddle says.

industrial

It's cool hearing about one interesting invention after another, but my mind keeps drifting back to YouTube. What kind of screen name should we have? Will we get a lot of subscribers? What if we don't get any views?

invention

subscribers

Talking at lunch earlier, Carly didn't have to say it, but I knew what she was thinking. *Is this just another one of Derek's crazy ideas or will he have the follow-through to make it happen this time?* I can't say I blame her; it's something I wonder about too.

assembly

interchangeable

But as I half-listen to Ms. McCoddle discuss the assembly line, I get an idea. What if we ASSEMBLE something on our YouTube show? Not like a desk from IKEA but things that don't usually go together—like ham and marshmallows or chicken soup and Jell-O? Maybe Umberto's right and we should do a challenge channel.

Ms. McCoddle smiles when she finishes talking about Eli Whitney and interchangeable parts. "Derek, you're grinning from ear to ear—is all this talk of innovation making you happy?"

I mumble something about Eli Whitney being one of my favorite inventors of all time, but even as the words leave my mouth, all I can think about is making videos with my friends.

# EXPERIMENT #1

Matt and Umberto don't need any
convincing to come over after school
to discuss our show. Carly's got an
orthodontist appointment so she
can't join us. That's actually good;
we'll be able to get all our bad ideas
out of the way while she's not here.
Because Carly's worried that she'll
have to get braces, I reassure her
that everything will be fine, although
I have absolutely no idea if she'll

orthodontist

refrain

need them or not. Matt tortures her by finding a website of people with terrible, gigantic braces, which almost makes Carly cry. In the end Matt feels bad, but not bad enough to refrain from sending a few of the pictures to her on Snapchat.

"Here's what I think we do," Matt says. He points to all the bottles and jars we've taken out of my refrigerator, now spread along the kitchen counter. "Let's find three of the most disgusting ingredients, mix them in the blender, then make ourselves drink it on camera."

"I still say eating handfuls of cinnamon and black pepper would be awesome." Umberto uses the deep voice he uses whenever he pretends he's an announcer at a monster-truck rally. "Master sneeze blast!"

I rub my hands together. "Time to mix up something vile."

vile

I take the cover off the blender and start dumping stuff in. Apple juice, maple syrup, canned clam chowder, a bagel, lettuce, and some blue cheese.

The three of us stare into the blender, looking down at the kaleidoscope of colors before turning it on. I take glasses out of the cabinet and divide the brownish mixture three ways.

kaleidoscope

"Whose idea was this, anyway?" Umberto asks.

"We should do this near the bathroom in case we have to puke," Matt adds.

We hold up our glasses in a mock toast then each take a sip before we gag. Only Matt finishes the drink and is declared the winner.

"I'm not sure if it's possible, but I think the bagel actually made it worse," I say.

"Not to mention the blue cheese," Matt adds with a belch.

tripod

"Um...Derek?" Umberto gestures to my phone set up on my dad's tripod. "Did you hit 'record'?"

We all look at the phone just sitting there.

"We're the worst youtubers ever," Matt says.

"So...take two?" I shrug as if this was all part of the original plan.

We obviously have a lot of work to do.

# BUSTED

Matt, Umberto, and I spend more time disagreeing than agreeing on what to shoot, so I'm not surprised that we don't have anything even close to usable when I go through the footage. It might be easier to do a few practice runs on my own. Mom's Derek-might-be-getting-into-trouble antennae must alert her, however, because ten minutes after

usable

Weimaraner

my friends leave she enters the kitchen.

She's wearing her scrubs with the Weimaraner pattern and looking at the counter full of jars and bottles.

"I hate to ask, but feel I should," she begins.

I tell her my friends and I were trying to come up with an idea for a YouTube show. Mom can't take her eyes off the mess.

"I'm surprised Carly was in on this," Mom says.

I could tell her Carly wasn't here, but since my mother thinks Carly walks on water, I decide to leave out this piece of information.

posterity

Mom points to the phone perched on the tripod. "Were you recording this for posterity?"

I'm not really sure what that means, but it doesn't matter because we didn't record much of anything. I tell her what we were attempting to do but with no success.

She opens the fridge and tilts her head. After a moment, I realize she's waiting for me to start putting the food away.

"I think a challenge channel is a great idea," she says. "The techs in my office watch them on their phones all the time."

The last thing I want to do is create a show that PEOPLE WHO WORK WITH MY MOTHER watch. But on the other hand, that WOULD get me additional views.... I just let Mom babble as I continue inserting jars of condiments into the shelves on the refrigerator door.

PUT TRASH HERE

inserting

"I bet a show about challenging yourself to be a better reader would really catch on," Mom continues.

I'm about to ask her if she's kidding but her slow smile tells me she is.

I've fought my parents on reading programs for years, finally coming up with one that works for me—drawing my vocabulary words in my sketchbooks to understand them better. I'm what's known as a visual learner, meaning I need to SEE things to learn them. I've done thousands of stick-figure drawings, which have definitely improved my reading skills. I know Mom well enough to realize she's not putting me down, just acknowledging all the hard work I've done since kindergarten.

acknowledging

Mom motions to the two jars in my hand. "Mustard or mayo? Paper or plastic? Truth or dare? Sometimes life just comes down to one thing or the other, right?"

Mom's semi-annoying observation gives me another idea. Instead of blending a ton of stuff together, what if my friends and I dare ourselves to complete challenges where BOTH options are disgusting? Would you rather have a booger sandwich or a dandruff shake? Would you rather go to school wearing your dad's pants or your mom's high heels? (Not that my mom wears high heels—she stands for many hours at work, so she usually wears clogs.)

disgusting

By the time the counter's cleared, I've thought of twenty revolting dares we can film immediately. I text my friends that it's time to make more videos.

revolting

With the camera on this time.

# TAKE TWO

uploaded

Now that Mr. Ennis is our teacher, we watch every video on his channel a million more times. In the episode he uploaded yesterday, he plays Latin music to a tomato plant until it gives him a cup of salsa to eat with his chips.

Carly, Umberto, Matt, and I watch it several more times before we begin today's filming. Mr. Ennis's editing is so seamless, no matter how hard we look, we can't see any signs of his cuts.

"Are we ready to shoot?" Umberto asks. He's got two hours until his van driver, Bill, picks him up from my house.

seamless

Mom's relieved we're not recording anything food-related and gives us her consent to film anywhere in the house as long as we clean up. It seems like a fair deal, considering my friends and I are still unsure exactly what we'll be shooting.

consent

"I like the whole 'Would you rather have choice A or choice B?'" Carly says. "I just don't want the choices to be gross."

unsure

"They HAVE to be gross," Matt answers. "Otherwise what's the point?"

I agree and hold up the clipboard with the list I came up with.

"Would you rather wear your best friend's underwear or use their toothbrush?" I ask the group.

Carly scrunches up her face, clearly unhappy with the way this is going. "Clean or dirty underwear?" she finally asks.

Matt and Umberto look at her like she's crazy. "Dirty, of course," Umberto answers.

"That's easy," Matt continues. "Use your friend's toothbrush. I use my brother's when I can't find mine— doesn't bother me at all."

"Yeah, but does it bother HIM?" Umberto looks to me. "Underwear, inside out—done."

"Should we turn on the camera and try to catch some of this magic on film?" I ask.

"Nobody uses film anymore," Umberto says. "Even blockbuster movies are shot on digital now."

blockbuster

"I know that!" Yet another friend who's a zillion times smarter than I am. Carly opts out of the challenge and decides to record us instead. I've got my cell hooked up to Dad's tripod and after modifying the height, Carly tells us we're good to go.

modifying

"Three .... two ... one ... action!" she calls.

Matt, Umberto, and I stand there, unsure of where to start.

Finally, Matt nudges me and I talk into the camera. "Hello, everybody! Welcome to the WOULD YOU RATHER challenge with Derek, Matt, and Umberto. This is our first video and I'm really nervous!" Spittle actually comes out of my mouth as I talk.

spittle

forthright

I HAVE A
BIG NOSE

apparently

Carly presses pause. "Should we try again?" she asks nicely.

Matt's a bit more forthright. "Derek, that was TERRIBLE! Are you trying to drown our viewers?"

"Then YOU go first," I answer. "We didn't even write anything down—I was winging it!"

"Should we make some cue cards?" Carly asks. "We can prop them up behind me on the couch so you can read them."

"I DON'T WANT TO READ CUE CARDS!" I shout at her. "I want to make a YOUTUBE VIDEO! IS THAT SO HARD?"

Carly picks up her bag and heads to the door. "Apparently, yes. See you at school."

I feel bad she's leaving, especially after our conversation this morning.

When I asked her at our lockers how it went at the orthodontist, she told me she has to get braces. Carly's one of the smartest, most fearless kids I know but she actually looked scared when we discussed it. Maybe I should've been a little nicer to her today.

I try to catch up with Carly but the only person in the driveway is Umberto's driver with the van.

Bill, Matt, and I help Umberto down the stairs in his wheelchair. Last time Umberto was here, Mom suggested getting a ramp that matches the one on the other side of the driveway for her patients. In all the times and different places Matt and I have lifted Umberto in his wheelchair, we've never dropped him. But I can't say I don't worry about it every time.

fearless

I go upstairs and drag Bodi out from his favorite spot—underneath my bed. Frank's in Mom's office, so Matt and I give up on our video and walk over to get him.

Nothing takes the edge off failure like hanging out with your pets.

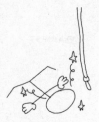

failure

# A CHANGE FOR CARLY

Lots of kids in our class have braces; it's not like getting them is a big deal. But Carly must be especially sensitive to having a doctor poke around in her mouth because she's in full anxiety mode today.

sensitive

anxiety

"The orthodontist says the first month might be painful." Carly looks ready to start crying outside science class.

"It'll probably only hurt for a few weeks," I say. "Think of all the ice cream you'll be able to eat before you can chew again."

My comment obviously makes things worse because a tear forms in the corner of her eye.

"You're tough," I tell her. "Nothing ever gets you down!" I have to admit I'm a little surprised at how difficult this is for her.

confesses

"I'm a baby when it comes to pain," she confesses. "Getting braces is all I can think about now."

My first thought is that maybe Carly will be so distracted by her braces that she won't be able to do her homework and I can get a higher grade than her—for once. But even I know taking advantage of Carly's anguish isn't what a real friend would do.

anguish

"It'll be like lots of things," I tell her. "It'll stink in the beginning but then you'll get used to it and it won't stink so much."

She smiles at my weak attempt at explaining how the world works and the tear in her eye doesn't fall down her cheek.

"You'll still be pretty," I say. "Even with all that barbed wire in your mouth."

apologize

Turns out that tear was ready to trickle down after all.

I apologize ten times but Carly ducks into the girls' room, successfully avoiding me to go cry.

avoiding

I can be such a moron sometimes.

# A SURPRISE

nosedive

The rest of the day isn't much better. I barely pass my English lit test, and Mr. Demetri took a nosedive into a mud puddle outside the gym and I missed it. (Matt DID get to see it and fell over laughing.)

YouTube class to the rescue! Not counting recess when I was little, I can't remember the last time I raced to anything at school.

"Welcome, welcome, welcome!" Mr. Ennis opens his arms wide like a ringmaster at a circus. I'm guessing he feels especially happy because the video of him making salsa already has a hundred thousand views.

ringmaster

I take my seat and notice the two empty spots where the Johnson twins usually sit.

"Melanie and Melissa won't be able to join us for the rest of the course," Mr. Ennis says. "I guess their dad's a bigwig in the computer industry and just got transferred to Palo Alto. Too bad—I thought they had a lot of potential."

bigwig

I stare at the empty desks. Two students on the class waiting list are going to be THRILLED. Matt and I nearly jump out of our own desks when Umberto and Carly enter the room.

"No way!" I shout.

Mr. Ennis just laughs; it's fun having a teacher who doesn't care when you yell.

When I last saw Carly she was crying, but now she's grinning ear to ear.

"Why didn't you tell me you got in?" I ask.

She shrugs like it's no big deal, when actually it's a gigantic deal. "I wanted to surprise you." Carly takes the seat closest to me.

grudge

I may have upset her a few hours ago, but one good thing about Carly—she never holds a grudge. With her and Umberto here, this class just went from amazing to off the charts!

"Today, we'll be laying the foundation for our own channels, so get out your phone or your notebook—however you take notes—and let's begin."

foundation

I pull out my sketchbook filled with hundreds of stick figures as well as notes for most of my classes.

"There are lots of steps you have to take to set up your own YouTube channel and the first thing you each have to do is come up with an original username," Mr. Ennis says. "There are millions of people already on YouTube so a lot of names have been taken."

When Matt pulls his desk over to mine, Mr. Ennis looks confused, then nods. "Everyone in this class is going to create their OWN channel. You may team up for projects in other classes but in this class, you'll be working alone."

Matt, Umberto, Carly, and I whip around to face each other. We've already put in so much work together!

Matt raises his hand. "How about if we WANT to work with someone else?"

Mr. Ennis laughs. "When I was your age, I hated working in pairs and groups. I was such a nerd, I always ended up doing all the work. Consider it a gift that you get to do your own thing."

harrumphs

setback

Matt harrumphs as he drags his desk back. Working alone is a definite setback but part of me is relieved. Some of Matt's ideas for our YouTube channel were good, but a few of them were definitely NOT my first choice. Bobbing for bologna instead of apples? Or challenging Bodi to a farting contest? Maybe getting to work by ourselves in this class will end up being okay after all. (Not that I tell the others; I put on a show and act as disappointed as they are.)

We all work on our own while Mr. Ennis scrolls through his phone, probably checking how many new views he has. Will any of us find the same kind of YouTube success he's found?

scrolls

I'm usually not much in the planning department—DUH!—but I've been giving my username a lot of thought.

"Okay," Mr. Ennis says. "Who wants to share?"

Matt's hand shoots up. "The UltiMATT Challenger!"

Mr. Ennis types into his phone so fast, it's like his fingers are caffeinated. "Already taken," Mr. Ennis answers.

"Super Girl," Carly volunteers.

"That's taken too."

Since there are a zillion people on YouTube, choosing an available username is harder than we thought. Half the class has to come up with different names.

"What about you, Derek?" Mr. Ennis asks.

slump

I slump in my seat, now unsure of what I've come up with. "Derek's Corner?"

"You asking me or telling me?" Mr. Ennis asks.

"Telling?"

Mr. Ennis laughs. "It's maybe a little—"

"Infantile?" Carly asks.

The rest of the class laughs and Carly shoots me a smile. I was worried the title might be a bit too *Sesame Street* and Carly just confirmed it. She's also doing something else—getting me back for making her cry this morning. Touché.

infantile

touché

stapled

Mr. Ennis takes a giant pack of stapled papers from his bag and starts to hand them out. "I planned to send you a PDF to save paper but your principal wanted me to hand out physical copies of what we'll be doing here too."

Tyler turns around in his seat to give me a handout as thick as that thing they used to call a telephone book.

"Turn to page one," Mr. Ennis says.

Everybody follows his instructions, but you can tell a few of us are puzzled because this is now beginning to sound like every other class in school.

"Before we get into what you guys will be doing on YouTube, we have to go over the things you *can't* do on YouTube."

I look down at the full-page list of restrictions.

"It even goes onto the back?" Umberto asks.

Mr. Ennis nods. "Everything you make here has to be one-hundred-percent original, G-rated, and approved by your parents before it goes online."

Gulp. I wasn't expecting so many rules.

"YouTube does not play around

restrictions

with material under copyright." Mr. Ennis continues. "If you use a popular song or clip from a movie or TV show without permission, not only will YouTube take it down, I'll remove you from class."

copyright

Suddenly I'm nervous. "How can anyone be creative with this much structure?"

structure

Mr. Ennis takes a seat on his desk. "You'd be surprised what you can come up with. All the videos on my channel obey the same guidelines I'm giving you. I also want to make sure your expectations are reasonable—I don't want anyone thinking they're going to end up an Internet sensation just because they're taking an after-school class in making YouTube videos."

I hate to pop Mr. Ennis's bubble,

pitfalls

viral

but every single kid sitting here thinks just that!

For the next half hour, he talks about the pitfalls he and his friends faced when they first started on YouTube. "We had sports channels, epic-fail channels, LP channels, fake-instructional channels—believe me, we tried EVERYTHING. I hate to say it, but there's a huge amount of LUCK involved. I know people who work their butts off, putting out quality content, and they've never gotten any recognition, and friends who shoot something in two seconds that ends up going viral. There is absolutely no way to know."

Shouldn't Mr. Ennis be giving us a pep talk instead of telling us what a downer YouTube can be?

He then goes into what he

expects from us in this class. We have to work on the layout of our channel—complete with banners and a logo—set up playlists of our videos, create a short trailer for our homepage, get a custom URL, schedule our uploads—not to mention creating tons of original content.

layout

It sounds incredibly exciting but I don't know how I'm going to have time to eat or walk Bodi, never mind keep up with my other classes. I guess that's the price you pay for fame.

"Then there are your viewers," Mr. Ennis continues. "You need to turn viewers into..."

He waits for someone to respond, and we all us do.

"Subscribers," we announce.

"That's the name of the game!"

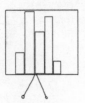

analytics

optimize

he says. "You need to engage with your viewers, answer their comments, maybe do a blog or newsletter, promote your channel on social media, share your videos outside of YouTube, study your analytics— in short, optimize your channel any way you can."

*In SHORT?* That sounds like *in long* to me.

"By next Friday everyone has to send me a basic outline of their channel, along with the rest of the details we talked about."

We all mumble, "Yes," and gather up our things.

"I can't believe how thick this handout is," I complain as we head to our lockers. "Even Ms. Miller doesn't give out this much work."

"We're making our own YouTube

channels," Umberto says. "Who cares how much work it is?"

Suddenly Matt starts laughing. The rest of us want to hear what's so funny.

"Derek's Corner?" Matt laughs. "Really? Sounds like story time at the library. You've got a LOT of work to do, my friend."

Back to square one—a place I'm pretty familiar with by now.

# QUESTIONS, QUESTIONS

2,000 EPISODES LATER

binge-watching

Mom is in the living room binge-watching a show on Netflix. She hits pause when she sees me.

"We need to schedule a call with Mary Granville from Helping Hands," Mom says. "Like it or not, we have to talk about giving back Frank."

She doesn't hit play, just waits for me to answer. I want to have a conversation about giving up Frank like I want to puncture my eardrum.

puncture

"Now?" I finally ask. "You're in the middle of a show."

"This can wait."

I pull out something I know she'll buy. "I have to do my homework."

She smiles. "Glad to see you're prioritizing," she says. "If it's not too late, we'll call her when you're done."

prioritizing

I stomp upstairs. I don't want to do homework. I don't want to talk to that lady. And most important, I don't want to give up Frank.

refuge

I take refuge with Bodi on my bed. Frank is a lot of fun but when it comes to comfort, there's nothing like lying next to your dog. My reverie is disturbed by texts from Matt, Umberto, and Carly all working on their YouTube assignments.

A message from Carly comes in. *Maybe we're just not cut out for YouTube.*

Umberto responds. *Oh, like a cat playing piano is? Or a rat carrying pizza? If ANIMALS can star in hit videos then we can too.*

Umberto's idea is GREAT. He's calling his channel Roll a Mile in My Shoes. It's a vlog where viewers will follow Umberto around while he goes to the store, to the beach, to the doctors. To people who can walk, that might seem like an ordinary itinerary but when you're in a wheel-chair, there are lots of obstacles to overcome. Wearing a GoPro, Umberto will act as a tour guide for the viewer to see what it feels like to be in a wheelchair. Talk about virtual reality! We text Umberto our approvals.

Matt is torn between doing pranks or comedy skits. For once, Carly can't decide what to do, going back and

vlog

MONDAY - PARIS
TUESDAY - LONDON
itinerary

forth between an unboxing show or a news channel. Usually she's the first one with a game plan but given the limitless possibilities she's surprisingly stuck. But who am I to talk— I am too.

unboxing

I shove my phone into my pocket and bury my face in Bodi's fur. Instantly, my muscles relax.

limitless

I don't know what I'd do without Bodi and Frank.

Hey . . . wait a minute! BODI AND FRANK. Most of the popular videos on YouTube feature ANIMALS.

I'm going to make Bodi and Frank YouTube stars!

# A NEW DIRECTION

badger

gold mine

Kittens, puppies, hamsters, an angry badger . . . they've all had millions of views. I've got a dog and a MONKEY—not to mention the thousands of other animals that go in and out of my mom's veterinary practice every year.

I'm sitting on a gold mine!

Matt goes nutty when he comes over that weekend.

"Your mom's a vet!" he says. "You can showcase a different animal every day. Does your mom have any sick hyenas? 'Cuz that would be AWESOME."

My mom, of course, would never in a billion years let me put any of her animal patients in my videos. I hate the thought of sneaking around her but we're talking about a future career here! Matt and I spend the next hour dunking chips into artichoke dip and brainstorming what kinds of videos I can shoot with Bodi and Frank.

artichoke

I've had Bodi since I was a toddler and he was a pup. He certainly is cute for a mutt. Frank, however, is a semi-trained capuchin who's very photogenic. Bodi is gentle and friendly; Frank is a downright ham.

photogenic

uncommon

Monkeys are a little more unpredictable than dogs, but they're also a lot funnier and uncommon too.

"How about if I record my voice and drop the audio in behind footage of Frank sitting at the table?" I ask. "It'll be like Frank is reading the news."

Matt shakes his head. "You have a MONKEY! Why do you want to put him at a table reading? He should be skateboarding or jumping off the roof!"

Matt and I have had the Frank-skateboarding discussion a million times. My mom would ground me for the rest of my life if she knew how many times Matt and I wanted to skateboard with my capuchin.

"Skateboarding's a no-go," I say. "But how about if we SHAVE him? A bald monkey would be hilarious."

"I thought the point was that your

mom DIDN'T find out," Matt says. "It would be fun to dye him with food coloring too but you'd still have the same problem."

Mom and I have talked about how people sometimes "paint" their pets with polka dots or stripes using paint that's not toxic, but Mom's not a fan of using an animal as an easel. Pet shaving and painting are definitely out.

toxic

"How about if he smashes stuff?" I suggest. "He can wear safety goggles and a lab coat and break things with a hammer? Then we play the video back in slow motion?"

"I'd DEFINITELY watch that," Matt answers. "Especially if he's smashing something messy."

"Like food?" I grab several handfuls of grapes from the bowl on the counter.

pulp

squashed

It takes Matt and me less than a minute to turn the fruit into a pile of green and red pulp.

"And that's just with our fists," Matt says. "Imagine what we could do with a mallet."

I scoop up the squashed grapes from the counter and throw them into the sink. "Wait—who's smashing things in the video? Me or Frank?"

Matt stops cleaning up and thinks. "Don't get me wrong—I'd love to watch you smash things. But you'd probably get more views with Frank, right?"

As much as I'd like to be the one on camera getting all the attention and having all the fun, a video with Frank would definitely get more views.

Looks like it's showtime for my capuchin.

# BATHROOM BREAK

My dad's been traveling a lot for work so it's fun to have him home this week. He's a storyboard artist in the movie industry and he's been on location in Toronto for a film about a superhero acrobat. As he takes the lasagna out of the oven, he tells us stories about the shoot.

acrobat

"There was a lot of tomfoolery on the set. The director had her hands full." Dad puts the lasagna on the

tomfoolery

counter to cool. Judging by the amount of steam coming out of it, we'll be eating dinner at midnight.

While we wait, we Skype Grammy in Boston. Mom likes to talk to her once a week and I do too. But Grammy's hearing is starting to go, so the conversation ends up with the three of us in California scream-ing into a laptop to someone three thousand miles away. Grammy shares her plans for a luxury vacation she's taking with two of her friends. I'm happy for her but in a while find myself staring at the lasagna and wondering if I'm going to have time to film Frank.

luxury

After we eat, I race to clean up the table then take Frank out of his crate. I'm hoping that Skyping Grammy doesn't make Mom realize that we still haven't scheduled that call with the woman from Frank's foundation. I clip Frank into his harness and take him upstairs.

harness

I gave a lot of thought to the smashing idea but eventually decided against it. Number one, I don't feel like cleaning up the mess every time I make a new video for my channel. Number two, it'll be pretty hard to hide the fact that I'm using Frank in my videos with all that smashing. In the end, I chose a much simpler idea: MONKEY IN A BATHTUB.

Sure, lots of other youtubers jump into bathtubs of Silly String, jelly, paint, slime, shaving cream— anything messy—but on my channel, a MONKEY's going to do it!

I prop my cell on the counter and crank up the music so my parents

extraordinary

can't hear what I'm up to. But given my mom's an alien from another planet with extraordinary antennae for trouble, she's immediately at the door.

"Are you taking a bath?" she asks. "Without being asked?"

I tell her I'm sweaty from PE and making myself sick with the smell.

"That's a first," she says. "I hope you're not thinking about taking Frank in the tub with you."

Is there anything mothers DON'T know? I tell her I'm not taking a bath with Frank, which is technically true because I don't plan on being in the tub with him. I wait for her to leave then undo Frank's harness and continue with my plan.

While I empty every bottle of Mom's bath stuff into the water,

Frank burrows into the dirty laundry in the hamper. I let him play for a bit while I finish setting up my phone.

burrows

When I'm ready, I scoop up Frank and suspend him over the tub.

"This is going to be fun," I say. "You LOVE to swim."

suspend

It's true that Frank usually loves the water but maybe because this is full of bubbles and smells like a forest, he's not sold on the idea. He gnashes his teeth the way he does when he's threatened or afraid.

gnashes

You don't need a mom who's a veterinarian to figure out submerging a capuchin into a bubble bath probably isn't the smartest of plans, but having stupid ideas has never stopped me before.

"Come on, Frank—the water's

submerging

fine!" I check the camera to make sure it's filming.

"You better not be up to any monkey business in there," my mother calls from the hall. "No pun intended."

I roll my eyes and let Frank scramble up my arm and onto my shoulder. If I'm going to make Frank a YouTube star, I'm going to have to film when my parents aren't home. I pull the plug on the tub and the water starts to drain. Luckily for me, tomorrow is Thursday Night, Date Night.

I'll just have to convince the babysitter that I ALWAYS film my monkey doing crazy stuff on Thursday nights.

# SOMETHING NEW

Even Matt thinks my new plan is impractical—and that's saying something.

"There's no way that can work—especially if Brianna's at your house," he says.

impractical

Matt doesn't need to remind me of the time we told my babysitter we baked her a cake, when what we really did was pack several sponges into a pan and spread them with frosting to make it LOOK like a cake. Brianna was NOT happy when she took a bite of our chocolate surprise. (My parents weren't too happy when they found out either.)

"You can film Frank at my house while your parents are out," Matt suggests. "Tell them you're sleeping over."

I shake my head. "Number one, it's a school night and they won't let me. Number two, Frank wasn't too happy about taking a dip."

Matt holds out his phone and shows me the footage he shot last night for his new LP show. It looks polished, with his face in the corner of the screen, commenting on Steve's movements in his Minecraft video.

polished

"It's not original, but I had fun," he says. "I'm still looking at other ideas too."

As Matt debates various options, I watch Carly approach us from the other end of the hall. Something's different about her, but I can't tell what it is. Then it hits me; Carly ALWAYS smiles—at pretty much everyone. Now her lips are pursed and her eyes are looking downward, which can only mean one thing.

pursed

She got her braces.

Before I can tell Matt not to joke around, Carly comes over.

"Don't say a word," she says. "My teeth really hurt and I'm not in the mood for wisecracks."

Matt smirks and starts to open his mouth until he sees the look on

Carly's face, which is so intimidating he immediately shuts it.

She turns to me and slowly opens her mouth, exposing more metal and rubber bands than I've seen in one place, outside of the vintage Erector set Grammy gave me several years ago. I COULD make a joke; however, Carly looks so awful, I don't have the heart.

"I'm sorry it hurts so much," I say. "The pain should go away soon, right?"

Carly shrugs. "One of my teeth is impacted, so it might be uncomfortable for a while."

"I wonder how those braces will photograph on your new YouTube channel?" Matt asks.

Carly looks like she's about to shove Matt into his locker. Instead

vintage

impacted

she takes the high road and just leaves.

"That was mean," I tell him. "Why make her feel worse than she already does?"

"She's always so perfect," Matt answers. "It's about time she has something we can make fun of."

When we get to math, Carly's seat is still empty. She finally comes in just as the bell rings and I can tell she's been crying again. I shoot Matt a look to make sure he doesn't make fun of her anymore.

Even if Carly WEREN'T one of our best friends, it's not cool to hit someone when they're down.

# SKETCHING WITH DAD

It's a good thing I hadn't planned on shooting my video while my parents were on their weekly date because one of Mom's longtime patients—a dog named Kitty—just got hit by a car and Mom is operating to save his life. Dad understands and they postpone their date a week to celebrate an early Valentine's Day. Now Dad's making us breakfast for

postpone

dinner and helping me with my homework.

"Remember when you'd only eat pancakes when they had Mickey Mouse ears?" he asks.

"Yeah, when I was two," I answer.

"You have a selective memory," he laughs. "I hate to tell you, but you demanded mousey-cakes until you were in third grade."

demanded

"I did not!" I can't help but laugh when he slides two mousey-cakes onto my plate. I'd never admit it in a thousand years, but pancakes DO taste better this way.

When my math worksheet is done, Dad asks about the YouTube class. I tell him I'm still not sure what I'm going to do for my channel. I DON'T tell him I was having a problem on set with my actor.

"Your mother and I were convinced you were trying to film Frank last night," he says. "You realize that wouldn't be a good idea, right? He's not a performer for your amusement."

I try and tell him I would NEVER do that, but Dad's not buying it. I finally give up and tell him I'm stuck.

"Some of those YouTube channels are spontaneous and unscripted," he says. "But some are very planned out. You might want to think about storyboarding your show first."

I smile because Dad thinks storyboarding is the answer to EVERYTHING. Over the years he's tried to get me to storyboard my homework, presentations, even Mom's surprise party. I don't mind drawing all my vocabulary words, but now I'm

unscripted

HERE'S KEITH!

supposed to illustrate my YouTube show as well?

"Just something to consider," he says. "You're a lot like me and I always think better with a pencil in my hand." As if to demonstrate, he grabs his sketchbook off the counter and starts drawing.

demonstrate

I love watching my dad sketch; he's lightning-fast, and even with a rough draft, you can always tell who or what he's drawing.

He holds up a drawing of me with a mouthful of pancakes.

"I'll give it a try," I say. At this point I'll take all the help I can get.

I spend the next hour sketching alongside my dad, which is my definition of a pretty great night. We talk about the movie set he's been on and his friend Doug who runs a prop company and just celebrated his fiftieth birthday. It's great to talk about Dad's life for a change instead of dissecting mine all the time.

When Mom comes in later, we both can tell by the look on her face that the surgery didn't end well.

Dad gets up from the table and gives her a hug. "You tried your best," he says.

mourning

She nods in agreement but I can tell she's mourning the loss of her patient. Dad pours them two cups of tea from the kettle while Mom sits beside me to look through my drawings.

kettle

She points to one of the pictures. "You didn't tell me Carly got braces!"

Until my mom said that, I hadn't even realized I'd been drawing pictures of Carly.

# BRING IN THE PROPS

Dad's storyboarding technique actually helped a lot. After all these years, you'd think I'd realize the best way for me not only to learn something, but to THINK about it, is with a pencil in hand. Illustrating thoughts for my new YouTube channel thrust me into a whole new level of ideas. (I won't use the pheasant jumping out of a helicopter—even if it did make

thrust

pheasant

me laugh out loud while I was drawing it.)

I've been spending 99 percent of my time thinking about Mr. Ennis's class, but I still have my other classes to worry about. (Not that I ever really WORRY about any of them.) I finish my assignment for science, then blast through my math problems as fast as I can. After an hour, I'm finally ready to tackle my YouTube work.

established

We're almost three weeks into the curriculum and I still haven't established what I'm doing for my channel. I decide to do some research, which basically means watching videos.

I check out challenge videos, instructional videos, prank videos, DIY videos, educational videos, and lots of wannabe rappers. Nine o'clock. Ten o'clock. Eleven. Twelve. Mom checks on me and I pretend to be asleep, but as soon as she closes the door, I dive back under the covers with my phone to watch another clip.

The next day at breakfast I'm so exhausted, I can barely keep my head off the table. (Mom's made her mixture of nuts, oats, and dates that she thinks Dad and I like but we just tolerate.)

mixture

The good news is, I know what I'm going to do for my show. IF Dad will help me.

"Remember when you told me about your friend who runs the prop company?" I ask.

"Of course I remember—it was last night."

I don't tell him that I watched so

many videos between then and now that it seems like a century has passed. "Do you think he'd let me borrow a few props to use on my YouTube channel?"

Dad takes a sip of coffee and thinks for a moment. "They're shooting a big Western now so you couldn't have those. But I'm sure Doug could lend you some props that weren't being used."

If I had more energy, I'd jump out of my seat. After my talk with Dad last night, I realized that as much as I'd like to use Frank in my videos, I'd be in for a heap of trouble if I did. If I have to star in my own show, having killer props will definitely set me apart from the crowd.

"BUT," Dad continues, "movie

costly

props are costly—you'd have to treat

them with the utmost care. I'm seeing Doug tomorrow—you want to come?"

I thank Dad profusely then shove my books into my pack and grab a lift to school.

Hopefully some movie magic will rub off one of those props and onto me.

# SO MUCH STUFF

fraternity

divorce

On Saturday, Dad takes me with him to meet Doug who has all the props. He and my dad have been friends since college, where they were both members of the same fraternity. Doug's been married three times and is going through another divorce, so Dad warned me not to ask Doug any personal questions— as if I was going to. All I want is to get my hands on some cool movie props.

When we get there, Doug's examining a shipment of the most lifelike skulls I've ever seen.

shipment

"That's because they're REAL." Doug takes one of the skulls from the top of the box and hands it to me.

"Just because we're in the movie business doesn't mean we don't use the genuine article when we can get it," Doug continues.

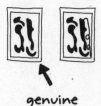
genuine

I've dissected frogs in Ms. Miller's class before but this is the first time I've held someone else's head. I hadn't planned on today being so hands-on—literally!

"Don't get any ideas for your video." Dad points to the label on the box. "Those are from a museum."

I carefully hand the skull back to Doug.

"From what your dad told me, you're not really sure what you're looking for. Why don't you stroll through the aisles and see if anything inspires you?"

It's an offer no kid could refuse. We're still at Doug's desk but already I can see rows of aliens, costumes, toys, bikes—it's like someone's garage, overflowing with a million things to rummage through. My mom LOVES yard sales; if this stuff was for sale, she certainly would've come with us instead of running errands.

errands

Doug asks me if I want some water or juice but I can't wait to start poring through these shelves. He gives me a giant cart—even bigger than the ones at Home Depot—and tells me that Jerry, one of his interns, will accompany me. Jerry barely looks up from texting but I don't complain, because I know that even with a chaperone, this is a tremendous opportunity.

chaperone

I'm not interested in any of the dishes or glassware but I'm impressed with how they've sorted everything by color, size, and shape. Every object is neatly labeled; now I understand why so many people work here.

I don't really care about the aisles and aisles of clothes either but the hats are a different story. Rows and rows of bowlers, fedoras, army helmets, aviator hats—I wish I'd known about this place back when I used to run around in costumes all the time.

fedoras

I take a turban off the shelf and ask Jerry if it's okay to try it on.

Jerry barely looks up as he nods.

I can't find a mirror so I use a nearby medieval helmet to see my reflection. Maybe I can tell fortunes on my YouTube channel!

"You're not thinking about dressing up like a fortune-teller, are you?" Jerry asks. "It's been done a thousand times."

I tell him OF COURSE I wasn't thinking of that and place the turban back on the shelf. Why does this guy have to be so negative?

Dad and Doug catch up to me in the room with all the nautical props. (After the intern's comment on my fortune-teller idea, I don't even THINK about doing a submarine show.)

nautical

"You need some help brainstorming?" Dad asks. "This place can be a little overwhelming."

I assure him that I can definitely come up with something on my own.

Dad points to his wrist where his watch used to be even though he uses his phone to tell time now. "You've got another half hour," he says. "After that, we let these good people get back to work."

I'm not sure if this snobbish intern falls into the "good people" category, but I realize Doug is helping us and I don't want to take advantage of the favor. I tell Dad I'll meet him at Doug's office soon.

As I wheel my empty cart into the next aisle, I can't help but let out a yell. Jerry looks up from his phone and nods.

snobbish

taxidermy

interviewing

"The taxidermy section always freaks people out," he says. "Especially the lion. We call him Walter."

I reach out to touch the gigantic creature. Of course, I know it's not alive but the creature is posed like it's ready to pounce and it takes a few moments for me to adjust.

"I think Walter might be too big for your school project," Jerry says. "Although it would make for a funny talk show interviewing a lion sitting on a couch in a TV studio."

Number one, it's more than a "school project." Number two, please stop coming up with ideas for MY YouTube channel. Number three, I am not going through rooms and rooms of props so I can have a stu- pid TALK SHOW! I don't share any of this with Jerry, just focus on all the animals, one more realistic than the next. (I compare the stuffed pheasant to the one I drew jumping out of a helicopter recently. My version was pretty good, if I do say so myself.) I also take a million pictures, which I immediately post to Instagram and Snapchat.

Believe it or not, something more impressive than the lion makes me grind the cart to a halt. A petite woman is carrying a humongous set of barbells, tossing them around like they weigh as much as a feather duster.

humongous

"Is she a famous bodybuilder or something?" I ask Jerry.

bodybuilder

Jerry looks up from his phone. "Sophia? She can barely open a jar. Those are fake weights."

Jerry must be getting bored with babysitting me because he shoves his phone in his pocket and leads me over to the shelf.

lightweight

"Everything here is made to look heavy but is really lightweight—the barbells, the medicine balls, the beer kegs, even the rocks. They use these in movies all the time."

Before he finishes talking, I'm loading items onto the cart. I can lift a boulder over my head! I throw an anvil into the air—and catch it! If Doug lets me borrow all this stuff, I'm going to have the best show on YouTube; there are so many ways I'll be able to use these!

The cart is really full. It takes me a while to maneuver it to the front of the warehouse. Doug nods in approval when he sees my choices.

"Ahhh, the magic of moviemaking." He picks up a giant boulder and hoists it over his head. "You should have some fun with these."

While Jerry makes a precise list of every item I'm taking, Dad makes his own list—of how I have to be 100 percent responsible for each prop, how each of them would cost a lot of money to replace, how Doug is doing me a favor, blah blah blah. It's usually the kind of speech I tune out but because I'm so eager to start making content, I listen and agree to everything Dad says.

On the way home, he continues in suggestion mode by recommending that I storyboard the show before I start shooting. This time, I don't even pretend to listen because I'm thinking about setting up my camera the second we arrive.

precise

responsible

# PRE-PRODUCTION

fiddling

placement

It takes a lot of fiddling around but after several tries, I finally figure out the best placement of the camera. Then I dig out a fake mustache from the Halloween box in the garage and slick my hair back to create the look for my new on-screen weight lifter—THE TANK. The joke is that in real life, I'm a skinny kid with barely any muscles, but with these fake weights it'll look like I'm lifting three hundred pounds. I test out a few different accents but decide to just use a lower version of my regular voice. A gray hooded sweatshirt, gym shorts, and sneakers round out my character's outfit. As I rehearse in my room, Bodi's not sure what's going on and eventually crawls underneath my bed to get away from all the action.

rehearse

The beige walls of my room make a boring background so I ask Mom if there are any old bedsheets I can paint to make a backdrop. She rummages through the hall closet and gives me a sheet from when I was little, covered with clouds and turtles. When I tell her I need a plain sheet, she finds a peach one for me to use. Peach isn't the ideal color for a bodybuilder but when you're scrounging for props, you can't be

backdrop

scrounging

fussy. She helps me hold the sheet up while I tape it to the wall to paint it.

"You need a drop cloth," she says, "so you don't get paint everywhere."

It takes a while to get the room ready and even longer to paint the words and background. I don't care if this is WAY more work than just talking into a webcam—I'm determined to have one of the best videos in class.

determined

Teachers and parents have always told me how creative and imaginative I am, however those qualities are unfortunately difficult to measure in school. I do well in a few subjects, but since so many of them involve reading, it's often hard for me to keep up with the rest of the pack. I can look at a globe and easily tell latitude from

latitude

longitude, yet seeing those words in a textbook is a different thing altogether. This YouTube class is a way for me to shine, so I take my time making sure everything is perfect.

longitude

After spending hours on pre-production (that's what they call it in the business) I'm ready to shoot. The actual filming takes less than an hour, but when you add it all up, this is much more time than I usually spend on homework. I'm relieved when I play back the video and laugh out loud at how ludicrous I seem. With some minor edits, I can tell by looking at the first pass that I've got a winner.

Even though I'm exhausted, I toss and turn all night, excited to show off my work tomorrow.

# VIEWING PARTY

eclipse

demons

At school the next day, all Ms. Miller can talk about is the upcoming eclipse. I guess in ancient times, people used to freak out when the moon suddenly disappeared and thought demons were involved. She makes us write down what time it will occur so we can see it, but as soon as she says it's at 3:00 in the morning, I just move my pen across my notebook as if I'm writing it down but don't. There are plenty of things worth waking up for in the middle of the night, and watching the moon play hide-and-seek isn't one of them.

Umberto skids over to me in the hall. "Wait till you see my vlog," he says. "It came out GREAT."

I do a double take—Umberto's now sporting a GoPro camera on his head like Mr. Ennis. I wave to the camera and make a bunch of stupid faces until he tells me the camera's not on.

As we head to class, Umberto skids to another halt when we spot Mr. Ennis. His long blond hair is gone, leaving nothing but a shiny bald head—and his headband with a camera.

scalp

vanquished

unwelcome

He runs his hand over his scalp. "It was a spur-of-the-moment decision. I'm still getting used to it."

Umberto and I try not to stare; when Matt joins us, he bursts out laughing.

"You look like Lord Voldemort!" Matt says.

"Then prepare to be vanquished!" Mr. Ennis smiles before he goes inside but the look in his eyes tells me even though he's joking around, Matt's comment was an unwelcome one.

"You realize you just insulted the guy who's grading us," I remind him.

"My video's primo," Matt answers. "I could run him over with my skateboard and still get an A."

"Highly doubtful," Umberto says.

In the room, the class asks another

fifty questions about Mr. Ennis's hair before we finally get down to screening our videos.

Mr. Ennis had us upload our clips to his Dropbox so he's got them all cued up to project onto the screen. Carly sneaks in later, apologizing that she had to hand in an assignment for another class. Carly is the school queen of extra credit.

The first video we watch belongs to Dave. In it, he's sitting at his kitchen table reviewing a new Netflix show. His comments are actually interesting, but every other word is *ummm*, which gets kind of annoying. He goes on and on about how terrible the Netflix show is. Is it weird to say that his horrible review makes me want to watch it?

"Wow," Mr. Ennis says when the

scathing

clip is done. "That was one scathing review."

"The show stinks," Dave says.

Mr. Ennis asks Dave what else he plans to review and if he's going to concentrate on a specific genre.

"I just want to find the worst shows and trash them," Dave says.

"It's easy to be critical of others but more challenging to create original content," Mr. Ennis says. "Why not try to be more creative with your show?" Mr. Ennis points to the soda can and bag of chips in front of Dave in the video. "You trying to get some kind of product-placement deal?"

monetize

"I want to monetize everything I can," Dave answers.

Mr. Ennis laughs. "Only a small percentage of the millions of people on YouTube make any money. Believe me, I should know." He hits play on the next video, which is Matt's.

"Strap yourselves in for a wild ride," Matt says.

I wait for the video to GET wild, but it's pretty much Matt sitting at his laptop doing a run-through of an old Crash Bandicoot game.

run-through

Matt turns around to watch the glazed eyes of his audience. "Come on, guys," he says. "It's really hard to get to that level!"

glazed

I proudly cheer on-screen Matt as he clears another level in the game, although my fake enthusiasm can't hide the fact that Matt's content is the worst thing anyone can say about a YouTube channel—it's BORING.

Mr. Ennis is kind with his feedback, giving Matt tips on how to spice things up a bit.

"But it was good, right?" Matt asks.

Mr. Ennis rubs his head for the hundredth time. "Sure."

Matt slinks down in his chair. I hadn't anticipated such a tough crowd either.

The rest of the videos are a lot like the ones we already watch on YouTube. Abby did an instructional video on French-braiding your hair.

generator

Barry made a meme generator with animal backgrounds that was hilarious. Candace shows us her advice channel dealing with a new step-mother, but she's so nervous on-screen, she looks more like someone who NEEDS advice than someone who should give it.

Umberto blows everyone away with his footage of trying to cross the street in his wheelchair when someone carelessly parked their car in front of the sidewalk ramp.

carelessly

Since being friends with Umberto, I've often put myself in his place as he maneuvers through the world, but I'm not sure the rest of the population thinks about all the obstacles someone with a physical disability has to go through every day. His video is a keeper for sure; Mr. Ennis even fist-bumps him before moving on.

population

I suddenly wonder if Mr. Ennis is taping our videos with the camera on his head as he's watching them. He wouldn't make a magic video out of our rough cuts, would he? Or edit them with boos and people throwing garbage at the screen? Between the bald head and the camera, he looks like an overgrown Minion and I decide not to worry about it.

Next up is Tyler, who's doing a YouTube Poop channel. His clip is a mash-up of *Gravity Falls*, old black-and-white vampire movies, and a gazelle getting torn apart by a lion to the sound of SpongeBob's famous laugh. It's random and gruesome and weird. Everyone loves it, especially Matt, who's a huge fan of YTP.

"Okay, Carly," Mr. Ennis says next. "Let's see what you've got."

Carly gives him a thumbs-up. She's been very secretive about her YouTube channel, sharing only that she decided to do a vlog.

*Maybe I DO have a chance to be number one now.*

When the clip begins, I'm surprised

gazelle

gruesome

secretive

at how simple the setting is. My ban-
ner and props make her no-effort
background look dull. Since Carly
usually decorates everything from
lunch bags to lockers, it's strange
she decided to go so plain.

"I just got braces," she says into
the camera. "And I HATE them."
She clenches her fists in frustration as she talks on-screen. "I am
CONSTANTLY running my tongue
over my teeth like there's some for-
eign object on them—because there
is! I can't believe I'm going to have
this contraption on my teeth for
almost two years!" She hurls herself
on her bed and throws a tantrum
like a little kid.

clenches

*This is so stupid,* I think. *Why are
you talking about your braces?*

But when I look over at my

classmates, they're leaning forward in their seats, laughing.

"That's how I feel with mine," Natalie says from the back of the room.

"Me too." Tyler gives a huge smile exposing his own metallic mouth.

Mr. Ennis has to pause the clip. "Okay, guys, let's wait until the end for comments."

Back on-screen, Carly continues. "I hate not being able to eat caramels! They're my favorite food in the world."

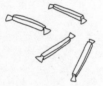

caramels

She starts fake crying and throws herself on the bed again. She looks as cute and smart as she does every day but I just don't get it—who's going to subscribe to THIS?

When the clip is finished, the

applause is greater than what the other videos got—even Umberto's, which was awesome.

Mr. Ennis turns to me. "You're up next, Derek."

I don't understand why I'm so nervous. I'm more scared now than I was in that play with Carly last year. I tell myself I worked hard and people are going to love it.

I hope.

# WHO'S THE DUMBBELL NOW?

"Helllooooo, it's me: the strongest guy in the world. Stronger than John Cena! Stronger than the Rock! I am THE TANK!"

reaction

On-screen, I'm lifting a giant barbell over my head. In the classroom, I'm not paying attention to the video as much as studying the reaction of the class.

No one's laughing.

"You're probably wondering how I'm lifting something so heavy," I begin.

"No, I'm not," Tyler says.

Mr. Ennis puts his finger to his lips, motioning for us to be quiet. "Let the video speak for itself," he says.

motioning

Back on-screen I juggle three oversized bowling balls as I talk. When I turn to Matt, he gives me a thumbs-up. (He's always been amazed by my juggling skills.)

oversized

"Welcome to my new workout show: Bodybuilding with THE TANK. The first thing we're going to do is some stretching."

stretching

On-screen, I bend down to touch my toes.

"You should've totally added a farting sound there," Matt says.

critiquing

Everyone laughs, even Mr. Ennis. I can't believe my best friend is critiquing my video!

I'm about to respond but Mr. Ennis points to the screen, where I'm lifting an anvil over my head. I squint and struggle under the weight, which in reality is only a pound.

"You can do it," I tell my viewers. "Grab some weights and work out."

The class is quieter than after Mr. Demetri gives bad news on the PA system.

"Tune in next time for more exercises with THE TANK!"

Mr. Ennis pauses the clip then puts his hands over his head, as if gathering his thoughts.

Before he can say anything, I jump in. "It's an instructional video like you said we could do. But it's also funny." I turn to the rest of the class. "Don't you guys want to know how I lifted such heavy stuff?"

"They're props, right?" Carly asks. "Not real barbells."

"Yes, but they look like real anvils, bowling balls, and weights, don't they?"

Carly seems confused. "But they're not—or you wouldn't have been able to lift them over your head."

"That's why it's funny!" I turn to Matt and Umberto, hoping one of them will take my side.

"I thought they were real," Matt says. "It was incredible."

incredible

Even I can tell Matt's lying.

"Here's what concerns me," Mr. Ennis says. "You never know who's going to click on your videos. Someone could watch this video, think it's a real exercise show, try to copy you, and get hurt. We talked about making responsible videos in our first class— I'm not sure this one is."

*Why is everyone missing the point?*

"The background is great," Umberto says. "Really nice lettering."

"Nice lettering?! I worked hard on that video!"

harmful

"We can see you put a lot of time into getting expensive props and building a professional set," Mr. Ennis says. "I'm just not sure a potentially harmful exercise show is the way to go."

sliver

Why did I think that just because I'm kind of creative my work would automatically be good? After years of being at the back of the pack, I had the tiniest sliver of hope that I'd be able to ace this class. Will there ever be anything I'm good at in this world? Because school certainly isn't one of them. I thought even I couldn't mess up a YouTube video, but I guess I was wrong.

Riding back home, the only thing Matt and I can talk about is class.

"The good news is that we BOTH have to reshoot," I say.

reshoot

"We're two of the funniest kids in school," Matt says. "How did we end up with the lamest videos?"

I tell Matt his video wasn't lame— just a little boring.

"Same thing," he argues. "But yours was definitely lame."

I skid my skateboard to a full stop.

"How is lifting three hundred pounds lame?"

Matt doesn't stop, just yells as he passes me on his board. "It looked fake."

Which is worse—boring or fake? All I know is that I don't want to be either.

I jump on my board and catch up to him. "Of *course* it looked fake—it WAS fake."

"I know that," Matt says. "You couldn't lift that much weight if your life depended on it."

"That was the JOKE!"

"I thought jokes were supposed to be funny." This time Matt's the one who pulls over on his board. "I'm as surprised as you are that Carly's video was the class favorite, but you have to admit, it was real."

"I wish someone had told me that's what we should be going for."

Matt tugs at his hair which he's growing out. "There are a million directions to go in, with no way to know what's going to work. Your video could've been the one everyone loved—it just wasn't."

I've been wondering something since we left Mr. Ennis's class. "But what if OTHER people like my video?" I ask. "Just because no one in class did doesn't mean that EVERYONE will think it's lame."

Matt agrees. "There could be some kid in Argentina who thinks it's the funniest thing he's ever seen."

snort

I laugh so hard I snort. "One kid in Argentina? That's the only viewer I get?"

"Don't feel bad," Matt says. "My only viewer is probably some

medication

grandmother in Kansas who found my channel by mistake."

"She was trying to buy some medication online, made a typo, and accidentally found your channel."

"The thing is," Matt says, "she leaves really thoughtful comments. She's improved my game tremendously."

Matt and I continue to make our silly stories even more ridiculous, and just like that we both feel better. We still have work to do, but we're entertaining ourselves and making each other laugh—which is what our videos were supposed to do.

# TODAY IS WHAT?

Dad's not too happy that I don't want to use his friend's props any-more. He tells me Doug gave us a lot of time and that I should make another attempt to use them before bringing them back after just a few days. Unfortunately, I'm determined to come up with something fresher and more original than the Tank. As we load the barbells and bowling

attempt

balls into his car to bring back to Doug, Dad loosens up a little and we pretend we're being crushed by all their weight as we lift them. It's stupid and funny and neither of us can stop laughing. I wish my classmates had thought my stunts were half as funny as Dad does.

When I get to school the next day, it becomes evident that something out of the ordinary is going on.

evident

Maria and Perry are both wearing dresses, and they NEVER wear dresses. Teddy's hair is actually combed and Matt is wearing a

blazer

BLAZER. And there's only ONE day a year that Matt gets dressed up.

Class picture day.

Matt gestures to my striped shorts and T-shirt. "What's with the outfit? Did you forget again?"

"You know I forget half the stuff

McCoddle tells us in class." My mother's going to KILL me. Just like last year.

Umberto slides up in his wheel-chair, looking as dapper as Matt. "Maybe everyone will think you're just one of the cool kids who doesn't care how they look in the yearbook." He and Matt exchange glances, then burst out laughing. "Nah."

dapper

The only person who looks unhappier than I am is Carly. She's got on a plaid skirt with leggings and a black T-shirt and looks kind of cute. But the expression on her face is pure anxiety.

Then I realize why. Her braces.

"I could have postponed getting these a few weeks until after picture day! Why didn't I look at my calendar?" she complains.

Carly stops ranting as soon as she

sees what I'm wearing. "Oh no—did you forget again?"

"Kind of."

A slow smile creeps across Carly's face. "That makes me feel the tiniest bit better."

Matt pulls the collar of his shirt. "Let's get it over with so I can take this stupid jacket off."

photography

hunched

The lady from the photography studio is set up in the gym. She looks pretty old, hunched over and with thick glasses. She must be trying to disguise the fact that she's ancient, because her hair is dyed jet-black with an inch of gray roots showing where her hair is parted. She's barking instructions to an assistant as she points with an arthritic finger to each kid in line. The bent fingers remind me of

arthritic

Grammy, who has arthritis too, but I've never seen a scowl like this on her.

scowl

Matt couldn't look more uncomfortable if he tried.

"At least I'll be relaxed in MY picture," I say. "Not pulling at my clothes like you."

He looks like he's about to smack me then suddenly starts laughing. He points to my surfing T-shirt with the migrating birds. "Your shirt is green."

migrating

"So?"

He points to the large green screen set up underneath the basketball net. "You can't wear anything green in front of a green screen!"

He's laughing so hard, Tyler and Umberto stop talking to listen in. I get it; Matt's just trying to take the focus off himself. But does he have to make fun of me to do it?

"I guess you didn't read the e-mail," Umberto says. "There are six different backgrounds to choose from. They insert them after they shoot us in front of the green screen. Don't you remember from last year?"

"Like that's the kind of information I remember!" I'm starting to really get annoyed with my friends.

"Hey!" Tyler yells. "Derek's wearing a green shirt!"

The news spreads down the line faster than if we were all playing telephone. Suddenly I'm glad I'm wearing green—it'll hide how sick I'm starting to feel.

Carly moves up the line until she's

beside me. "It's okay," she says. "No one cares about these stupid pictures anyway."

Sure, Carly's trying to make me feel better but all this attention is making me think I'm REALLY going to get sick—with my luck, just as this cranky lady snaps the photo.

cranky

Carly, unfortunately, is now the target of my pent-up irritation. "Thanks for the update," I respond. "I hope the photographer's lights don't bounce off your braces. It might look like you've got lasers shooting out of your mouth."

Matt's talking to Maria but runs over when he hears me. "Does this mean we can finally make fun of Carly's braces? I've been saving up a million insults!"

Before I can answer, Umberto

does. "No, we are NOT making fun of Carly's braces."

Carly whips around to face me. "Are you sure? Because it certainly sounds that way to me."

I feel bad that I'm the one who started this whole thing and just want this line to finally move so I can get out of here.

chants

"I'm sorry," I tell Carly. "You look great for your photo—really cute."

"Ohhhhhhhh," Tyler chants behind me. "Derek likes Carly! Derek likes Carly!"

He stops when Carly glares at him, crosses her arms, and faces down Matt and me.

$2 + 2 = 5$

inaccurate

"If you think you're going to send me running to the bathroom to cry again, you're wrong, inaccurate, erroneous, mistaken, misguided— you want me to keep going?"

Matt and I stare at the parquet floor and shake our heads. It stinks having a friend who's a billion times smarter than you are—especially when she's angry.

parquet

Even though I ask her to stay, Carly goes back to her place in line with Natalie.

Umberto lets out a low whistle. "That girl is a thesaurus! She thrashed you—and for good reason, too."

thesaurus

If I had a dollar for every moronic thing I've ever said to Carly, I'd be able to buy a plane ticket TO FLY ME ANYWHERE BUT HERE. I'm actually relieved she stood up for herself; I'd feel horrible if her picture came out bad because of me.

thrashed

It doesn't take long before I'm first in line. I comb my hair with my hand and hope for the best.

"YOU!" the woman yells. "Stand on the X. Now!"

I do as I'm told and hurry to the spot on the floor marked with two pieces of duct tape. Behind me is a large screen of green fabric, pulled tight. Three large studio lamps have been lighting up this spot for hours; I hope this woman takes the picture before I start sweating through my shirt.

"The instructions said NOT to wear green," she says.

I mumble something about forgetting, even though I never read the email.

"It's your funeral," she says.

"My funeral?! Isn't that a bit extreme?"

And just as my face is scrunched up and puzzled, she clicks the camera.

"Hey!" I say. "That's not fair! You have to take another one!"

"One per student. Next!" The woman points to a large table with several sample photos. "Pick a backdrop—not that it'll matter with that shirt."

Why did they hire this lady? Why can't we have some cool, NICE photographer instead of a tyrant?

The backdrop choices are totally boring—swirly gray and brown, bricks, a grassy field, a wall of books.

swirly

At this point it doesn't matter what I chose. I select the wall of books as a joke—that no one else will get since I'm never showing this picture to anyone.

# AN ANNUAL EVENT

incident

This weekend is the annual street fair that everyone at school's been talking about for days. All I can think about, however, is Tuesday's incident with Carly. Over the years we've had plenty of arguments, and in the end, we always end up okay. This time she hasn't responded to any of my texts, which has me worried. I even called her last night—and

I never make voluntary phone calls—but it went straight to voice mail.

voluntary

I hate that feeling you get when things are off with one of your friends. It's like you're wearing a shirt that doesn't fit. You feel tight and uncomfortable all day, no matter what else is going on. I've been looking forward to the fair but hope I can still enjoy it with this weird feeling inside.

The street fair doesn't start until eleven, so I've got time to hang out before walking over with my parents. Both my parents are good cooks but neither of them can compare to having lunch at a food truck. There'll be grilled cheese trucks, lobster trucks, taco trucks, ice cream sandwich trucks, Korean BBQ trucks—how are you supposed to choose?

I know I should eat a small break-fast but I wolf down two bowls of Cinnamon Toast Crunch while watching TV with Bodi and Frank.

"SMC?" My dad sticks his head into the living room. SMC is our acronym for Saturday Morning Cartoons—something Dad and I came up with when I was little. I enjoyed cartoons back then—DUH!—but still haven't outgrown them. I don't plan to, either. Maybe it's because paying attention in school all week is so difficult, but by the time Saturday comes around, sitting on the couch with my monkey, dog, and a giant bowl of cereal is the perfect antidote to all that work.

Mom's new thing is slathering coconut oil all over her hair so her

Too Much
INFORMATION
↓
TMI

acronym

outgrown

antidote

head's wrapped up in a towel when she sits down with her coffee. Hydrating your hair seems pretty unnecessary to me. I don't have to do anything to mine and it gets oily on its own.

hydrating

"I talked to the director of the capuchin foundation about Frank," she says.

As if he knows he's being discussed, Frank moves from his place on the couch to Mom's lap.

"Can't we talk about this later?" I ask. "There's nothing worse than hearing bad news while you're watching cartoons."

Mom sips coffee then smiles. "It's actually *not* bad news. Their training classes are so full that she gave us an extension. Frank can live with us for another six months."

extension

Hearing this makes the strait-jacket of anxiety I'm wearing loosen up the tiniest bit. I jump up from the couch, grab Frank, and swing him around like we're dancing. "That's great!"

"Better than thirty food trucks?" Mom asks.

"Better than a hundred food trucks!"

agonizing

Over the past few weeks, every time I started to think about Frank leaving, I pushed the thought out of my mind. I know Frank has to go someday but I've gotten so attached to him, it's going to be agonizing to say goodbye. Six months may not be forever, but it's better than losing Frank now.

"You've done a good job working with Frank since he's been with us,"

Mom says. "You two have really bonded."

bonded

Frank definitely does have some kind of sixth sense, because he looks up at me with this expression so full of emotion it almost looks human.

Mom grabs her phone from the pocket of her robe and snaps a picture. "That's a keeper."

She holds the phone up for me to see. Frank and I look like a film poster for a cross-species buddy movie.

When Mom checks the time, she tells me we'll be leaving for the street fair in an hour.

I suddenly wonder where Bodi is and it doesn't take me long to spot his two paws peeking out from underneath the curtains. I scoop him up in

convoluted

my arms and settle back on the couch for some more SMC with the two greatest animals in the world.

The whole way to the fair, Dad tells this convoluted story about one of the women in the costume department who got transferred to a different job because she kept shrinking the actor's clothes when she washed them.

He's acting out all the people in the story with different voices and sound effects, but as we walk toward Wilshire the only two things I can think about are if Carly will text me back and finding a new idea for my YouTube channel that doesn't include barbells. Maybe there'll be a performer or vendor here who'll ignite my creativity.

vendor

ignite

The line at the Korean BBQ food

truck snakes around the entire park-
ing lot. The lines at the chowder
truck, the taco truck, and the Philly
cheesesteak trucks are almost as
long. NOOOOO!

"Want to get a salad with me?"
Mom points to the veggie food truck
with only three people in line.

"I'M NOT GETTING A SALAD AT
A FOOD TRUCK!" I shout so loud
that a mother with two kids in a
stroller turns and gives me a dirty
look. So does Mom.

"Come on, let's get some sliders,"
Dad says. "That line is long but
manageable."

manageable

We each use our phones while we
wait. (Carly still hasn't texted.) When
it's our turn, Dad orders turkey patties
with cheese and I get the bacon and
mushroom sliders. The baby burgers

don't take too long to come out; even so, by the time we find Mom, she's already finished eating.

There are lots of people here from the neighborhood and several of Mom's patients. It's nice to see them, but I'm on the hunt for inspiration and end up walking ahead of my parents.

inspiration

Moon bounce? Too young.

Face painting? Too messy—AND too young.

Adopt-a-dog? Already have one.

When I double back to see what my parents are up to, I find Mom at a booth learning how to make soap with herbs and olive oil. She ends up buying several kits to make her own lemon and lavender soap, which is probably good since I used up all her bath stuff trying to film Frank.

lavender

Dad just shakes his head. "She's

never going to use those—you know that, right?"

I laugh, knowing how enthusiastic Mom gets about arts and crafts projects, forgetting she doesn't have a lot of extra time to do them in.

Dad tries on a few T-shirts and buys one with a minnow swimming against the tide. I don't really get it, but he seems happy so I am too.

minnow

"You want to get something?" he asks. "There's a vintage Pac-Man there."

Usually I'd take advantage of some cool free stuff but my attention is fixed on a guy in the next booth putting handfuls of earthworms into a bucket. He sees me looking at him and motions me over.

compost

"Did you know you can start a compost heap with worms in your backyard?" he asks. "They'll eat your

fertilizer

food scraps—even coffee grounds! The garbage passes through their bodies, making a rich fertilizer you can use in your garden."

Mom peers over her reading glasses into the bucket. "I wonder if Carly's mom knows about this."

Carly's mom's a landscaper and their garden is full of the biggest birds of paradise I've ever seen. Maybe Carly's mom uses GIANT pooping worms.

Mom asks the guy more questions until Dad drags her away. "Making your own soap AND composting?" he asks. "Are we quitting our jobs now?"

Mom ignores him, moving on to the leather sandals in the next booth.

sampling

Dad LOVES sampling food—it takes forever to get him out of Costco, where he tries bite-sized pieces of everything from cheese to salmon. Today is no different. Spoonfuls of blueberry honey, multigrain bread on a toothpick, and sausage in a little paper cup—Dad's not fussy when it comes to trying new foods.

salmon

"Try this hot sauce," he tells me. "It's got ten different chilies—it'll blow a hole in the back of your skull."

Mom shakes her head and walks away; she's not a fan of spicy foods like Dad and me who'll put hot sauce on just about anything.

Dad hands me a piece of bread doused with a sauce called Taste Bud Explosion 10.

"It makes our Taste Bud Explosion 9 seem like baby formula," the vendor tells us.

The sauce has barely hit my mouth when I start sweating. The vendor doesn't blink, just hands me a glass of water. If I were a cartoon, there'd be steam coming out of my ears with fire engine sound effects. I still can't talk but give my dad a big thumbs-up.

He takes out his wallet and reaches for two bottles of the hot sauce. "It'll kick our chicken chili to a whole new level."

premise

But I'm not thinking about chicken or chili or even nachos. I just figured out the premise of my new YouTube show!

# YET ANOTHER IDEA

My parents have been adamant about me not using Frank in my YouTube videos, but considering the class reaction to the Tank, I don't have a choice but to go back to using my capuchin. I'm facing some fierce competition—not just from the other kids in Mr. Ennis's class, but from the billions of people already on YouTube. Anybody with a monkey

adamant

disobey

at his or her disposal would use it, right?

Even if I'm going to disobey my parents, I know better than to give hot sauce to a monkey. Of course that doesn't stop me from putting a tiny drop of the new hot sauce on my finger and letting Frank lick it off when we get home. He seems to like it—even tries to grab the bottle out of my hand—but if I'm going to shoot lots of videos, I'll need a substitute for Taste Bud Explosion 10.

gratefully

Gratefully, Mom's meeting a friend and Dad's catching up on work so the chances of them cutting into my fun are slim. I rummage through the back of the fridge where all the half-eaten jars of curry and pickles are until I find a bottle of hot sauce from the last street fair or farmers' market Dad went to. I empty the contents into the sink, rinse the bottle, and refill it with ketchup, a harmless condiment that will look exactly like hot sauce in the video.

Frank must know something's up because he's already clambering to get out of my arms. As soon as I douse one of his monkey biscuits in ketchup, Frank grabs it out of my hand and gobbles it down. I squirt some ketchup on the outside of the bottle to keep him interested.

clambering

Capuchins are pretty good at foraging, so my idea is to hide the bottle of hot sauce and have Frank root around the house to find it. In post-production, I'll speed up the footage, add cartoon sound effects,

foraging

as well as a theme song to make the video even funnier. So question number one: Where should I hide the hot sauce first?

Inside the fridge, the vegetable bin is full, so I bury the bottle underneath the lettuce, zucchini, and carrots. Frank's on my shoulders, bouncing in anticipation. I make him wait a few more minutes as I set up my cell on the tripod.

When I'm finally ready, I prop open the door of the refrigerator so Frank can have full access—and I can have light to film. He doesn't wait for me to turn on the camera, just starts shoveling out the vegetables until he finds the bottle. I constantly try to get Frank to look into the camera but he's pretty focused on finding his snack.

zucchini

focused

By the time he's finished, the floor of the kitchen looks like a produce stand. Frank's gotten ahold of the fake hot sauce and is guzzling it down and squirting it on the vegetables. I scoop all the veggies back into the bin so my parents won't find out.

guzzling

Before I put Frank back in his crate, I snap a picture of him holding the bottle of hot sauce and text it to Carly. She might still be angry with me, but she's always had a soft spot for Frank.

My phone immediately dings with a new text.

It's from Carly. *A picture of you with hot sauce is NOT an apology.*

I type back. *That was Frank, not me. Besides I apologized WITHOUT hot sauce too.*

I watch the three dots bouncing on the screen as she types her reply.

Come on, come on!

*Are you sure? Looked more like you than Frank.* Then the school emoji and a wave goodbye.

Yes! I am forgiven!

Cleaning up the kitchen after that is a breeze.

forgiven

# READY, SET, GO!

I can't wait to show Mr. Ennis and the rest of the class my new video. Unfortunately, I've got a full day of school to get through before that.

Islam

There's a test in social studies on Islam; I tried to study for it but spent too much time with hot sauce and ketchup instead. I know three out of the twenty questions and end up guessing the rest. Mr. Maroni tells us we'll be starting the section on

Buddhism

licorice

Buddhism next week—maybe I'll have better luck with that religion.

When it's finally time for Mr. Ennis's class, Matt and I race down the hall until Ms. Cardoza in the media center gives us the evil eye. I almost slam into Carly, which is weird for a moment—are we still good?—until she hands me a stick of red licorice and tells me to stop clogging the halls. Yup, things are back to normal.

In the past week, Tyler made more than ten YTP videos—all of them wacky and ridiculous. He always kept a low profile so I'm kind of surprised his work is head and shoulders above everyone else's. I guess all the time he's spent watching YTP has paid off when it comes to making clips of his own.

Umberto's video is also funny—but unpleasant to watch at the same time. In the clip, he's at a restaurant on the Promenade with his brother, getting ready to have lunch. When the waitress comes over, she only talks to Eduardo, asking him what Umberto will have too.

unpleasant

I've been in those embarrassing situations with Umberto before—when people talk to Matt or me instead of Umberto as if he's just his disability and not one of the smartest, funniest kids on the planet. It's not that strangers should KNOW he is; they just should give him a chance. This time, Umberto kindly—but firmly—lets the waitress know that HE'LL be having the chicken tacos without the cabbage but with lots of sour

cabbage

cream. When the clip ends, Umberto gets even more applause than Tyler.

Throughout the class, I keep glancing over at Mr. Ennis, who looks as mischievous as I do before Brianna comes over to babysit. He's got something up his sleeve but I can't figure out what it is. (A pizza party after class would be AWESOME.)

As Mr. Ennis cues up Carly's video, she leans over in her chair. "Don't freak out," she whispers.

Alarm bells go off in my head. "What am I going to freak out about? I don't freak out."

"Yes, you do!" Carly points to the screen where her video is starting.

tiresome

I guess she's still doing that tiresome show about her braces because she's sitting in her room talking on webcam again.

"Talk about bad timing," on-screen Carly begins. "I got my braces the week before class picture day! I felt ridiculous! Should I smile with my teeth and flaunt my braces? Or smile with my mouth closed which feels totally unnatural?" She then runs through several kinds of smiles for the camera—some of them are funny, some are cute, and a few are downright scary.

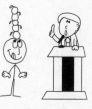

flaunt

unnatural

When I look over at Matt to see what he thinks, he's staring at me and making a cut-your-throat motion with his hand. I mouth, "What?" since I have no idea what he's talking about. He just shakes his head and looks back at the screen.

"So I've got swollen gums, I feel ugly, and the photographer is mean—and as if THAT'S not enough—two of my best friends start making fun of me while we're in line! You heard me—two of my best friends!"

I look around the room, hoping everyone doesn't know who she's talking about, but pretty much everyone does and is staring at Matt and me. Carly just shrugs as if she's not the one who made the video.

Throwing herself on her bed and pretending to cry must be a running gag on Carly's channel because she does it again now. At the end of the class, she gets as much applause as Umberto and Tyler.

"Well," Mr. Ennis says. "Any comments?"

I don't even bother raising my hand. "You said we were fine," I tell Carly. "Why'd you have to make that video?"

Carly looks at me with an expression that's not mad, just serious. "I think a better question is, why'd you have to insult me in the first place?"

It's a good point but it doesn't answer my question. "I know all our channels are still set to private, but you wouldn't post that if they were public, would you?"

Before she can answer, Mr. Ennis jumps in and asks the rest of the class if THEY think Carly should post it.

"Totally!" Natalie says.

"Absolutely," Tyler adds.

Umberto looks torn but joins in anyway. "I think sometimes the uncomfortable videos are the ones that hit the hardest."

Mr. Ennis says it's time to

move on to the next video, but before he does, he asks Carly what she'd do.

She doesn't hesitate. "I'd totally post it."

thoughtless

Great—make me look like a thoughtless moron just as our teacher is about to screen my new video. Thanks, Carly.

But I don't need to worry— Monkey Love Hot Sauce is a hit. I'm glad I decided to speed up the video and add sound effects; it makes Frank's search for hot sauce even more frantic and silly. Mr. Ennis laughs out loud which puts a cherry on top of the class reaction.

"That was great, Derek," he says. "See what you can accomplish even with all those rules and parental supervision? Your parents did sign off on this, right?"

I can't tell Mr. Ennis that I was the one who scribbled Mom's signature on the parental permission form, so I just nod and tell him they liked the video too.

scribbled

"Frank's a star," Tyler says. "Please say you're using him in all your videos."

Getting one good video has taken much more time and energy than I'd planned on. But after all those practice attempts, I finally came up with something that works. As I tell Tyler I'm definitely using Frank again, all I can think about is how I'm going to hide my shooting schedule from my parents.

Next up is Matt's video, which has been shrouded in mystery. All

shrouded

he's told me is that he gave up the LP idea in favor of something different.

Before Mr. Ennis hits play Matt turns to the class and tells us he decided to do an unboxing video.

WHAT?!

If you'd asked me to bet on what type of YouTube channel Matt would create, unboxing would be at the very bottom of the list. Most of the unboxing channels consist of a woman with fancy nail polish opening toys while her disembodied voice talks to you like you're a two-year-old. Please don't say Matt's going to do THAT. Unboxing a new smartphone or even a bag of Doritos is more like Matt. I'm confused—and curious— to see what he's come up with.

On-screen, Matt is dressed like a

disembodied

caveman; I recognize the outfit he's wearing as his mom's sheepskin rug. His face is dirty and he's sitting in the woods—which I also recognize as a trail we've hiked in the Santa Monica Mountains. Did he use a tripod or did someone else tape it? Does he have another best friend now? I decide to stop worrying and just watch the clip.

His caveman character holds an old cardboard box painted gray, fastened with a piece of jute. Matt put a lot of work into his video too; I guess coming up in the rear of the class taught both of us a lesson last week.

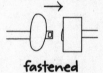

fastened

jute

"Welcome to Shopping with Neanderthals. Today, we're going to see what's in this package I just picked up at my local StoneMart."

Several kids laugh, including me.

Caveman Matt unties the string and slowly opens the box. As he does, he's swatting imaginary flies.

swatting

"Ohhhhhh, look at this." Matt slowly lifts a large rock out of the box and holds it up. "This one's a beauty. Nice shape, good grip. I'm going to be able to clobber lots of other cavemen with this bad boy." He weighs the rock in his hand. "They really made some improvements over last year's model; even the packaging is better."

packaging

He signs off with a grunt and we all applaud. Matt beams, happy that he came up with something funny and original. He tells us his brother Jamie helped him, which eases my fear about a new best friend.

After all the videos are shown, Mr. Ennis tells us he has a surprise. NOW can we have some pizza?

"As of today, you can all move your YouTube settings from private to public so everyone can finally enjoy these beauties."

Wait—everyone in the WORLD is going to see Carly talking about how mean Matt and I were?

"From here on in," Mr. Ennis says, "you'll be promoting your channels and uploading new videos. And remember: It's not just about views and subscribers—it's about creating videos you can be proud of."

As much as Mr. Ennis says it's not about numbers, I don't have to ask my classmates what they'll be aiming for because I already know the answer—views. Umberto, Matt,

Carly, and I originally thought we'd all be making videos together. Now I have to compete with not only everyone in the class, but my best friends.

# BAIT AND SWITCH

Several kids in our class already have lots of videos "in the can," which means shot and ready to go. I, on the other hand, have to film all the new Monkey Love Hot Sauce videos from scratch.

As I lie in bed Saturday night, my mind is abuzz with everything I have to do. Film the videos, edit them, upload them, promote them, answer

**abuzz**

comments ... then start all over again. Is this what it feels like to be a grown-up—a constant stream of stuff you need to accomplish? If it is, I'm not in any hurry to sign up.

Even though today is Sunday, Dad has a meeting and Mom's next door interviewing for a new recep- tionist, so I'm clear to start filming the next episode of my channel. But first I need to come up with a theme song!

It's been a while since I used GarageBand, so it takes me over an hour to make a song I'm happy with, one that feels panicky and fueled by hot-sauce energy. I turn on the lap- top's internal mic and record the theme song to my new channel.

*Monkey love hot sauce!*
*Monkey love hot sauce!*

*It's so hot, I love it a lot!*
*Monkey love hot sauce!*

It's ridiculous and stupid—in other words, perfect for YouTube.

I don't know how long Mom's going to be working, so I have to hurry if I'm going to film Frank. Where should he go kooky for hot sauce today? The TV room? The trash?

kooky

Within the next few hours, Frank scours my mother's jewelry box, the recycling bin, as well as a basket of laundry, and the washing machine. The only difficulty Frank had was with one of Mom's bangles. He was in such a frenzy to get his hands on the hot sauce that he ended up with the bracelet caught around the lower part of his face. It made for hilarious footage but he started

scours

bangles

tangled

freaking out, so I had to stop being cameraman/director and help him. A few of my mother's chains and necklaces got pretty tangled, so I put them back in the bottom of the jewelry box where she won't find them for a while.

By the time I get Frank in his crate, he's exhausted and passes out on his blanket. Then I look for Bodi. I can't give him equal time tonight, but I need to at least give him some. I settle him next to me on the couch as I download the footage from my phone to my laptop.

The footage came out GREAT and I'm excited to get to the editing phase, until I realize I've forgotten something. Since I can't show my parents Monkey Love Hot Sauce, I'm going to need a decoy channel to

decoy

show them what I'm doing for class. I not only have to make Frank's show, I need to make another whole fake channel. What's THAT show going to be?

I look around the room and bat around ideas. Derek eats? Boring. Derek eats candy? Been done. Derek watches TV? Too passive.

passive

Mom's got a few boxes near the front door of things going to Goodwill. She asked me a few days ago if she could get rid of some of my old toys and I said fine. I open up the boxes until I find the one full of action figures.

I really don't feel like working but there's no way around the task at hand. I set up the camera again and dump the box of action figures onto the kitchen table.

"Hi! Welcome to Action Figure Mashup," I say to the camera. "I'm Derek, your host, and we're going to create some NEW action figures out of my OLD action figures."

I don't have time for a lot of takes so I make sure to speak as clearly as possible. "First, we're going to take off Bart Simpson's head and put it on Gumby." I yank off Bart's yellow head and shove it onto Gumby's stretchy green body. "Ta-da!" I hold my new creature up to the camera. "Say hello to Bartby."

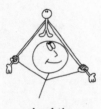

stretchy

I sign off then check the quality of the video as Mom enters the kitchen with a stack of folders. She pours herself a glass of wine and asks how filming went. I lean over and show her the footage I just shot.

She takes a sip of wine. "Do you

think it might skew a little young? You haven't played with those toys in years—you might get a lot of four-year-old viewers."

skew

I tell her I don't care WHAT age my viewers are, as long as I have some. But her comment makes me wish I could share my REAL show with her.

"See what your teacher says," she adds. "But I think you might be able to challenge yourself a little more."

She takes her glass and work upstairs and tells me it's time for bed.

She has no idea I'll be up for hours.

# THE HEADLESS
# HORSEMAN

remarks

In school the next day, everyone who takes Mr. Ennis's class is talking about how many views their videos have received, as well as some of the funny comments. Tyler's YTP site has lots of absurd remarks, which only makes sense. Umberto's are very positive, which makes sense too.

The real surprise is Carly's

channel; while the rest of us have single-digit viewers, Carly received more than thirty comments in twenty-four hours, even a few from people who DON'T wear braces. I check my channel between classes and at lunch, but only have seven views—all of them probably mine when I was testing it last night.

"The day you've all been waiting for," Ms. McCoddle says before she dismisses us. "Your class pictures are back."

Just what I need—MORE bad news.

There's lots of excitement as she hands the pictures out; I just hope that lady who took them was better with a camera than she was with people.

Ms. McCoddle stands in front of

**wavering**

**cranes**

decapitated

my desk, wavering. "I'm not really sure what happened here. Maybe you should sign up for the reshoot day next week."

She hands me the see-through envelope. I DON'T want to see it, but like an accident on the other side of the freeway, I can't help but look.

My head is suspended against a wall of books. Just. My. Head.

Matt cranes his neck toward my seat. "Dude! It looks like you were decapitated."

It doesn't take long before everyone is on their feet, mocking my head floating amid a backdrop of books.

I'm not sure if my parents will laugh or be annoyed that I didn't pay attention to the photographer's dress instructions. Either way, they'll insist I do a reshoot.

I grab my pen and write NO GREEN SHIRT on the back of my hand. Hopefully I'll remember to read it this time.

# NUMBER
# CRUNCHING

portrait

Both Mom and Dad think the class photo is hilarious; Mom even insists on buying it AND scheduling a makeup. She removes an old family portrait from the shelf above the TV and slips my disembodied-head picture into it. After all these years, I still can't tell when Mom will find something funny or not.

I end up working all night EVERY

night for the next week. Finding new ways for Frank to be obsessed with hot sauce, staging, filming, editing, adding sound effects, uploading, creating playlists, tagging them, tweaking the tags, responding to people who leave comments—who knew being on YouTube was so much WORK?

tweaking

Carly's vlog continues to get tons of comments; she's got the most viewers and subscribers of all of us, by far. It's actually infuriating because her videos take a few minutes to shoot, even less to edit, with hardly any pre-production. How can she put in the least amount of work and get the best results? I should realize by now that my accomplishments will NEVER compare to Carly's. Ever.

infuriating

Tyler continues to create bizarre YTP videos that have no point to them, which of course IS the point. Matt's channel is kind of a one-joke bit, but since he uploads a new video every week, he's gotten a few hundred subscribers. For someone who goofs off as much as Matt does, he is surprisingly focused. He hasn't said anything, but it makes me wonder if he might end up going into filmmaking for real.

We all knew Umberto's videos would reach a wide audience; there are other people doing accessibility shows on YouTube but none are as funny—or by someone as young—as Umberto's. I can't decide which of his videos is my favorite. I love the one where he's trying to order a smoothie but can't see over the

accessibility

counter because he's in his chair and the guy working there can't tell where Umberto's voice is coming from. I also like the one when his shirt gets caught in the mechanism of his wheelchair and he brings pedestrian traffic to a halt as he tries to remove it. I've been in the world with Umberto enough to know that he'll never run out of new material.

Monkey Love Hot Sauce is doing okay; I've had lots of great comments and proudly have 165 subscribers. But I barely sleep, barely stay awake through classes, and, most important, I'm so busy MAKING YouTube videos that I no longer have time to WATCH YouTube videos. Unless you count my own.

Is it weird to watch your own

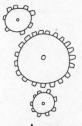

mechanism

pedestrian

177

videos to increase your views? Are the other kids in this class doing the same thing? Or am I the only loser in the bunch? These are the questions I'm too embarrassed to ask the others, even my best friends.

mystified

My parents seem mystified by what they think is my YouTube channel.

"So are you going to take these mash-up action figures and DO something with them? Some *Robot Chicken* kind of thing?" Dad points to the pile of figures on the kitchen table. He picks up half Batman/half Pikachu and walks him toward me.

*Sure, Dad, great idea. Why don't I create a THIRD show?*

Mom just shrugs at the pile of misfit toys. I can tell she's not impressed. I just want them both to go to bed so I can shoot more secret videos of Frank.

I DID have time to watch Mr. Ennis's new video a few days ago. In this one, his friend Chris joined him in the weekly digital magic show. Chris has set up a Slip 'N Slide in the yard and Mr. Ennis walks by in a tuxedo. Chris blasts Mr. Ennis with the garden hose and suddenly the tuxedo becomes a tuxedo-printed wetsuit. Mr. Ennis slides down the Slip 'N Slide and lands perfectly dry in his regular tuxedo again.

tuxedo

Carly's newest videos follow her same vlog format and you can see that the positive response she's received has made her even more confident. In one, she talks about having lunch with her cousins, then looking in the mirror later and

lunch meat

gingerbread

seeing her braces are covered in everything from lunch meat to gingerbread and how embarrassed she was.

"None of my cousins told me my mouth looked like the inside of a garbage disposal," she says on-screen. "Not one!" As usual, she throws herself onto her bed and fake cries. She ends the segment by saying she's putting up an AMA video next week. Mr. Ennis says Ask Me Anything videos can be fun but cautions Carly to make sure all the questions are appropriate before she answers them.

I'll be the first one to admit that I didn't get Carly's vlog in the beginning. But the more I see it, the more I understand why others are attracted to it.

People mostly watch videos for entertainment and to learn how to do something, but over the past few weeks, I've seen there are also other reasons. To connect with people or to feel like you're a member of a group. Without planning to, Carly created a forum for other kids to share their thoughts, feelings, and stories about having to deal with braces. And it's paying off.

forum

"Do you think we were wrong to just go for laughs?" Matt asks.

We're at my house where he's helping me set the stage for Frank to forage through the tub of old sports equipment looking for hot sauce. So far, I've spent half of my birthday-money savings on ketchup, which Frank has devoured.

equipment

"I just wish I'd done something

easier," Matt continues. "I have to get into my caveman costume, put on makeup, find something new to unbox, beg Jamie to drive me to the trail, then film me.... I hate to say it, but it's not as much fun as I thought it would be."

"You had me fooled," I say. "I thought you loved it."

"I did," Matt says. "But my channel's been up for weeks. That's practically forever in YouTube time. I thought I'd be a star by now, like Logan and Jake Paul or Jacob Sartorius—girls screaming, hit records, the whole thing."

"What bothers me," I confess, "is that it makes you realize how you're just a drop in the bucket—one of a zillion people posting videos every day. No one's sitting around waiting for us to post something, that's for sure."

"Do you think anyone in our class will get BIG?" he asks. "Superstar big?"

"I doubt it. The chances are minuscule for that kind of fame." I hide the bottle of hot sauce in the bin. "You're not thinking about SINGING online, are you? Because you have a terrible voice."

minuscule

"It's not about the singing," he says. "It's about the fans."

When Mom appears in the garage, I block the tub of gear and the hot sauce. The whole reason we did this today was because she wasn't supposed to be home until later.

She asks what we're up to.

"Just going through stuff." I hold

up my old baseball mitt, which is so small I couldn't fit into it if I tried. "Remember this, Matt?"

"We played a lot of baseball with that mitt," Matt agrees.

nostalgia

"I hate to interrupt the nostalgia party," Mom says. "Just wanted you to know I canceled my appointment and I'll be working here if you kids need anything."

She leaves—along with my plans for filming Monkey Love Hot Sauce today.

# ANALYZE THIS

"It's important to try and understand why some videos work and others don't," Mr. Ennis says in class. "Let's talk about Carly's latest video on her playlist and try to analyze why it already has 212,530 views."

WHAT? I had no idea Carly was bringing in those kinds of numbers. If I had numbers like that, I'd make sure the whole school knew.

He hits play as we watch Carly tell a story about talking to her mom when one of the rubber bands on her braces snapped.

"You'll never guess where it landed," she says. "In my mother's mouth! I mean, she's my mother, but still! Suppose it had been someone from school? OMG—suppose it was someone I had a crush on!"

*Does Carly have a crush on someone I don't know about?*

Mr. Ennis hits pause and asks us for feedback.

vulnerable

Natalie raises her hand. "Carly isn't afraid to be vulnerable. If you have braces, you can really relate to her frustration."

"She's cool and funny," Tyler adds. "I bet half of her subscribers don't even HAVE braces."

*Is Tyler the one she has a crush on?*

Mr. Ennis asks Carly if she's tried to figure out who her subscribers are.

"Sixty percent of them are girls," Carly says. "And in my rough calculations, approximately seventy percent of both boys and girls who leave comments wear braces."

calculations

*Is she kidding? Who does this kind of research on their viewers?*

"One girl—at least I think it's a girl, but you never know—is so cute, writing her own braces anecdotes in the comment section every single day. I actually look forward to Power73's thoughts."

Mr. Ennis is impressed with how much work Carly's put in to analyz-ing her data. "Today we're ALL going to look at our numbers." He pats his

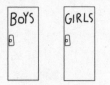

demographic

estimating

stomach like he just ate. "Guess what the number one demographic is for my channel, LOL Illusions?"

We all make different guesses, with most of us estimating Mr. Ennis's audience to be made up of kids and teenagers like us.

He shakes his head. "The biggest group of viewers I have are women over eighty. I have a huge following in the assisted-living community."

"No way!" several of us shout.

He laughs and shrugs. "You're right—it's kids your age. But wouldn't it be great to reach seniors too?"

He tells us to go to our YouTube channels and head to the Creator Studio. We follow his instructions and click *Analytics* in the menu on the left.

"You can also check your videos individually by clicking the Analytics button under each video."

A few kids in the class—Carly and Natalie—seem familiar with these pages but for the rest of us, this information is a revelation. How many people liked and disliked each video, how old they are, what kind of device they watched it on, how long they watched it, if they shared it, even how many times they watched it.

revelation

device

Mr. Ennis walks around the room as we study who our viewers are. He stops when he gets to my desk and points at the graph I'm staring at.

"For example," he says, "this shows that Derek had two hundred and twenty-three views on his new

shabby

| 12957 | 35961 | 96919 |
| 97869 | 12439 | 67198 |
| 89818 | 92321 | 47982 |

column

Monkey Love Hot Sauce clip from last night."

I puff up my chest a bit. Not too shabby!

"But what this column shows is that two hundred and twenty-one of them were from the same person." He looks at me and laughs. "I'm guessing that's maybe a grandparent who misses you?"

I can't let my classmates know I spent all last night clicking on my own videos to raise the number of views for today's class! I laugh and say my grandmother watches everything I post multiple times.

Mr. Ennis continues to study the chart then moves to another area in the menu. "Well, unless your grandmother is a twelve-year-old boy in Los Angeles with a smartphone, your enthusiastic viewer doesn't seem to be her."

Umberto and Matt start laughing hysterically.

"You're tweaking the stats by watching your own videos?" Umberto says.

Everyone laughs, including Mr. Ennis. I can feel my checks flush bright red.

"Okay, that's enough humiliation for Derek for one day," he finally says.

...AND THEN SHE SNORED SO LOUD I HAD TO SLEEP OUTSIDE BUT...

endlessly

It turns out Mr. Ennis is wrong because Matt, Carly, and Umberto remind me of it endlessly for the rest of the week.

Many, many times.

# COMMENTS

maximize

ratchet

We're all very aware that because Mr. Ennis's class is a weekly after-school elective, it runs for a shorter period of time than our other subjects. When I realize there are only three classes left, however, I go pedal-to-the-metal to maximize my number of subscribers. Matt, on the other hand, tries to ratchet up his views. Even though Mr. Ennis keeps telling us that views and subscribers are only one way to track YouTube success, my classmates and I spend a lot of time debating which is better—to have a lot of subscribers or to have a lot of views. In the end, I guess they're BOTH pretty important. Not that it matters much in terms of the competition, with Carly and Tyler so far ahead of the rest of us.

From studying the comments, I discover that lots of people really like my Monkey Love Hot Sauce theme song. A few people think I shouldn't be using a capuchin in my videos in case he gets hurt. (Frank getting stuck inside Mom's bangle drew several negative comments from people who were worried about his safety.) But on the whole, most people seem to really like my channel.

In class the other day, Mr. Ennis talked about the pressure to always come up with something new, having to best yourself and make every video better than the last. "At first, I was just pulling things out of pictures and books," he said. "Next thing you know, I'm climbing out of a mailman's pocket to surprise my mom on Mother's Day and jumping through subway cars without opening the doors." First and foremost he talked about making sure what you do is safe. I always try to be safe with Frank—no matter what people might suggest in the comments.

All this thinking about Frank makes me miss him, so I head to the kitchen to take him out of his crate.

foremost

Mom's cleaning up after dinner then sits down at the table with us.

She reaches over to pat Frank's head. "I thought Frank looked like he's been putting on weight, so I took him to the office to weigh him. He's gained three pounds in the past month—that's a lot for a capuchin this size."

I suddenly wonder about the caloric content of ketchup.

Frank leaves my arms and jumps into Mom's.

"You're not feeding Frank extra snacks, are you?" she asks me. "The woman at the foundation wants him to stay on a pretty specific diet."

I tell her I feed him the chopped-up veggies and fruits we're supposed to, along with his monkey pellets.

pellets

She holds Frank in front of her and talks to him in her baby voice. As a vet, she's professional 99 percent of the time, but once in a while the kid inside her pops out and she lets herself be amazed by how cute all these animals are.

"Who's putting on a little weight? Who is?" she coos to Frank.

Between Frank's unpredicted weight gain and Mr. Ennis's class coming to an end next week, it looks like I'll only be able to film one more Frank video.

It's got to be a showstopper.

showstopper

# RACE AGAINST TIME

My parents are next door at the Blakes', which should hopefully give me enough time to film.

After my conversation with Mom about Frank's weight yesterday, I decide to use something else besides ketchup and monkey biscuits to get him to go nutty over the bottle of hot sauce.

I take out the jar of mealworms

mealworms

delicate

piñata

from the cupboard where we keep Frank's and Bodi's food. But what should I put them in? Eureka! I place the dead worms in the mesh bag Mom uses for delicate clothes. Thankfully, the holes in the mesh are small enough to keep the worms inside. I hang the bag of worms and hot sauce from the dashboard of Mom's treadmill like a piñata that Frank will try to grab. Frank is really going to have to work for his hot sauce today.

"Okay, buddy," I tell him. "This is going to be fun."

Frank's as excited as I am and leaps onto the base of the treadmill. He immediately starts jumping to reach the bag. I lean over him to the dashboard and put the treadmill on its lowest setting. Frank doesn't miss a beat, just takes tiny steps and begins to run.

This time I don't use the tripod so I am able to move around and get some action shots that I'll edit into a fast-paced scene. Frank is doing great! He continues to hop up during his jog, striving to get those worms.

striving

Would it be bad to let a few of them loose on the treadmill?

I open the bag and take out some mealworms, filming myself as I do it. I dangle them in front of Frank who starts running even faster, trying to grab the snack. As he's about to, the worms fall out of my hand and roll into the guts of the treadmill.

A few dead worms can't break a big piece of machinery, can they?

I scrunch up my face, waiting for

grinding

the treadmill to come to a grinding halt, but it continues to move. To make sure it doesn't get stuck, I raise the speed a little. Frank runs even faster so I increase the speed a little more.

The next noise I hear is the outside door, telling me my parents are home. I shut off the treadmill, grab Frank, and duck into my room.

I forgot the bag of mealworms and hot sauce!

From the sound of their voices, my parents are at the bottom of the stairs so I race back to the treadmill and untie the bag.

*Come on, come on!*

untie

snatch

I don't have time to snatch the several mealworms that fall on the rug as I race out of there.

Seconds later, Dad opens the door

to my room. "You get all your work done tonight?"

I tell him I did.

"Why are you so out of breath? Exercising?"

He gives me a thumbs-up when I tell him yes.

Mom sticks her head in and tells me the Blakes say hello. When she sees Frank, she tells me to put him back in his crate. I tuck the bag of hot sauce and mealworms underneath my shirt and take Frank to the kitchen.

Frank seems exhausted from all that running so I sit at the kitchen table and hold him.

"You did a GREAT job," I whisper. "Now it's time for your reward."

I empty what's left of the bag of worms on the table and watch Frank scramble to eat them. If I'd thought about it longer, I would've taken my phone with me to get this on film.

"You deserve every one of those." I rub the top of his head then put him in the crate.

Upstairs, my parents are still in the hall. Mom's balancing in the doorway, taking off her shoes. "I couldn't wait to get these off." She turns to Dad. "Some yoga before bed?"

Dad agrees and takes off his shoes too. They say goodnight and head to their room.

squishing

The thought of mealworms squishing between my parents' toes during downward dog makes me want to gag.

I hope they're using yoga mats.

## YES!!!!!

The treadmill clip of Monkey Love Hot Sauce brings me over nine thousand views in the first twenty-four hours! Watching the number of views grow every few minutes makes me happier than the day we first got Frank.

Suddenly my number of views puts me in Umberto and Tyler's league. With only one class left, the chances of us knocking Carly out of first place are slim, but second place is still something to aim for.

A few of the comments are negative—"you're abusing that poor animal!"—but most people say they like it. The popularity of this clip must be carrying over to the others on my playlist because ALL my videos increased overnight; my subscribers are way up too.

quarterback

At school, I feel like a quarterback who just made the winning touchdown.

touchdown

"Dude!" Matt says. "That video is killer!"

"The sound effects and song really make it," Umberto says. "I laughed the whole way through."

So many pieces of music that I wanted to use were copyright-protected; Mr. Ennis talked about only using royalty-free music many times, so I knew he'd go nutty if I illegally downloaded a piece of music instead of buying it. In the end, I found a great piece of free music that sounds like the circus and really works.

When we get to class, Mr. Ennis and Carly are huddled at his desk. Wait—are they planning a surprise to celebrate my smash hit?

huddled

Mr. Ennis waits for us to take our seats. He must not have liked being bald because his scalp is now covered in stubble where his hair is growing out.

stubble

"We've got some big news." He bows toward Carly and asks if she wants to tell us.

Carly stands in front of the room and takes a deep breath. "Remember how I told you that I had one viewer who wrote to me every day? Power73? Well, it turns out her mom is a producer on *Ellen*."

Natalie and Bridget actually scream.

"And they're doing a segment on youtuber kids and they want me to come on the show!"

The rest of the class goes ballistic along with Natalie and Bridget. Ellen has a HUGE fanbase for her show as well as online viewers. Being on her show will launch Carly's vlog into the stratosphere!

stratosphere

I'm happy for Carly—that's GIGANTIC news—but can't we take ONE SECOND to acknowledge my big accomplishment? Am I doomed to follow in Carly's footsteps forever? Still, seeing how thrilled she is makes me realize I'm being petty

petty

and so I let out a hoot to celebrate Carly's windfall.

windfall

"There will be six of us and they're looking for one more kid to replace the Fine Brothers who had to cancel. Since I live locally, they asked if I had any recommendations on such short notice."

*I'm Carly's best friend! This is a slam dunk!*

Carly runs her tongue along the front of her teeth, a new habit since getting her braces. "I wanted to talk to Mr. Ennis first because I don't want to hurt anyone's feelings." She opens her arms to encompass everyone in the room. "I love all your work but I only get to pick one."

encompass

*I'm gonna dance with Ellen! I'm gonna dance with Ellen!*

"Umberto, do you want to join me on the *Ellen* show?"

Wait, what?

Umberto lets out a Tarzan yell. "Absolutely!"

Carly addresses the rest of the room, but she's mostly looking at me. "I think Umberto's vlog is really important and can make a lot of people aware of what people with disabilities go through every day. Millions of people watch Ellen's show—Umberto's videos can really have an impact."

impact

I obviously can't argue with Carly's thinking—it makes complete sense to choose Umberto. However...

"Maybe you can talk about some of OUR channels too while you're on," I suggest.

Mr. Ennis interrupts before Carly

can answer. "The focus will be on their two channels," he says. "But two out of six kids are from this school? That's incredible! You should all be proud of yourselves! It's also important to note that their channels weren't chosen because they had millions of views but because they connected with people." He turns to Carly and praises her again.

praises

Matt leans over and whispers to me. "Aren't you used to swimming in Carly's wake by now? I am."

He's right. But at least this time, Umberto will get some well-deserved recognition too.

recognition

After class, I'm halfway down the hall when Carly catches up to me. "I LOVE your channel," she says. "You know that. It was a really hard decision."

"I know it was."

She spins around to face me. "As funny as your channel is, I just couldn't waste the chance to make a difference."

Carly stands in front of me, waiting. I know she wants a smile and it only takes a few seconds before I give her one.

"I'm proud of you," I tell her. "You did the right thing."

She squeezes my arm and runs down the hall.

"When are you filming *Ellen*?" I call after her.

"Tomorrow!!" she yells back.

There are actually worse places to be than swimming in Carly's wake.

# NO!

My mom's going to FLIP when I tell her. She loves Carly and she loves Ellen so it's going to be twice the good news.

But when I step inside the kitchen, both my parents are waiting for me. Dad looks as mad as I've ever seen him; Mom looks incredibly disappointed.

On the kitchen table is Mom's laptop.

fishy

comprehend

It's open to Monkey Love Hot Sauce.

"I knew there was something fishy about your action figure mash-up channel," Mom finally begins. "I just couldn't comprehend why you were doing it and now I know why."

"Was that some kind of decoy so we wouldn't find your REAL videos?" Dad asks. "The ones you made with Frank that we told you over and over NOT to create?"

"You better start talking, and I mean NOW," Mom says.

"No one liked the videos I made of me," I finally stammer. "We live with a monkey! I had to use Frank!"

Dad tilts his head. "Even after we told you repeatedly not to?"

"There is not enough punishment to go around for this one," Mom says. "Not only did you betray our trust, you put Frank in dangerous situations."

"It wasn't hot sauce," I cry. "It was ketchup!"

"Frank is on a restricted diet! Do you know how much sugar is in a spoonful of ketchup?" Mom asks. "More sugar than a chocolate chip cookie! Frank could have diabetes now." Mom takes a deep breath, winding up for more.

Dad takes a seat on one of the kitchen stools. "I took you to Doug's, he let you borrow props, we signed off on every one of your decoy videos. We've been very supportive from day one. But you were deceitful with us, and it's hugely disappointing."

deceitful

"I didn't want to lie," I answer. "But I HAD to. The competition is

STEEP. Frank may be a few pounds heavier, but he's FINE. I'll take any punishment you want to give me for lying—and I'm really sorry you feel betrayed—but, everything's okay! Frank didn't get hurt!"

desperate

It's a solid pitch, even if my voice did sound like I was a little desperate toward the end.

"Derek, how do you think we found out about these videos?" Mom asks.

It's something I've been wondering since I walked in the door.

Mom answers her own question. "Mary Granville told me."

"Is she one of the techs in your office?"

Mom turns to Dad with an expression of disbelief before turning back to me. "Mary runs the foundation where we got Frank."

"Oh, the lady who said we could keep him—I remember."

"Yes, the lady who said we could keep him when she thought we were taking good care of him. Now she's the lady who thinks we're endangering him so she's hopping on a plane to take Frank back. She'll be here first thing Monday morning."

WHAT HAVE I DONE?!

endangering

# A HIGH PRICE
# TO PAY

defunct

The videos on my Monkey Love Hot Sauce channel have now reached 15,750 views. I have over 2,000 new subscribers. What my subscribers don't know is that they've subscribed to a channel that is now defunct.

My parents make me take everything off YouTube, even the decoy action-figure channel I'd set up just for them. They make me send an email to Mary at the capuchin foundation to apologize. Her response is immediate—she will still be here Monday morning.

Everyone in the entire school is excited about Umberto and Carly talking about their YouTube channels on *Ellen*, but it's difficult to get caught up in all the excitement when I only have a few days left with Frank.

Matt takes the news hard—he loves Frank almost as much as I do. I make the decision not to tell Carly and Umberto until after the *Ellen* taping so they're not upset during the show. Matt think's that's a mature thing to do, but mature is the last thing I'm feeling right now.

Mom and Dad go back and forth with the appropriate punishment.

privileges

sandwiched

Take away my phone? My laptop? Ground me? Take away my skateboard? To me it doesn't matter what they choose because all those things are nothing compared to losing Frank. (Yes, even phone privileges.)

When I get home from school the next day, I immediately take Frank out of his crate and hold him. Bodi won't leave our side, as if he knows something's about to happen, the way animals can sense a change in the weather. I pull them both toward me until I'm sandwiched between them on the couch.

I know I'll have to explain everything to Mr. Ennis, but right now the furthest thing from my mind is making videos. But who am I kidding? The videos weren't at fault—I was.

I guess Mr. Ennis was right when he talked about the pressure of creating the latest and greatest videos, having to top yourself each and every time out of the gate. Without realizing it, I got caught up in views and subscribers and beating the other kids in class. Maybe if I'd done something simple like Carly or helpful like Umberto or downright absurd like Tyler, I wouldn't be losing one of my best friends.

Dad comes in and plops down beside me. He holds out his arm for Frank, who climbs up it to sit on Dad's shoulders. "You're not the only one who's going to miss Frank," Dad says. "We ALL love this guy. It's going to be strange not having him around the house anymore."

I'd been so wrapped up in my own feelings that I hadn't thought about how this would affect my parents. Or Bodi.

"I'm really, really sorry," I say for the zillionth time.

"I know you are." He leans across the table, grabs his sketchbook, and starts drawing. Frank inside the window of an airplane. Frank reuniting with his capuchin friends back in Boston.

23 YEARS LATER

reuniting

"Does drawing Frank help make the pain go away?" I ask.

"I don't know," Dad answers. "I always think art helps, don't you?"

A slow smile spreads across my face.

Dad just gave me the BEST IDEA EVER.

pry

I reach up and pry Frank from my father's back. "Come on, buddy. We've got some work to do."

# A BETTER VIDEO

In hindsight, I should've done this from the beginning. But if your name is Derek Fallon, you usually take the long, windy road to success instead of the short, simpler one.

This time, I'm doing a vlog—but not for YouTube—for the lucky person who'll end up with Frank as a companion.

I start in the kitchen where I go

NOT MY BEST IDEA!

hindsight

mangoes

secure

through Frank's favorite foods—mangoes, bananas, sweet potatoes, and turnips. "But you have to make sure to chop everything really small to fit into Frank's hands," I say into the camera. "And if he doesn't like his monkey biscuits, you can soak them in orange juice and he'll eat them right up. He also really likes mealworms—but not too many at once."

Next, I go through how to clean Frank's crate and to make sure it double-locks. "Frank is VERY curious," I tell the camera. "If the crate isn't secure, he'll definitely be able to get out."

Dad comes inside from getting the mail and nearly drops it when he sees me filming. "Please tell me you are NOT posting videos of Frank again."

I shake my head and tell him what I'm doing.

His face relaxes. "That's a great idea."

With Dad as my assistant, the

assistant

rest of the video goes much faster—except the part about Frank's favorite movies and TV shows. I want to make sure wherever he is, Frank still gets to enjoy the Westerns he loves, so I really take my time.

In between shots, Dad and I talk about who Frank might end up living with next. A kid in a wheelchair like Umberto? An elderly woman who needs help getting things down from shelves? Someone with a spinal injury like our friend Michael? Whoever it is, Dad and I agree he or she will be lucky to have Frank.

After I edit the footage, Dad and

I watch the rough cut. I decide to go the extra mile and add some music, fun sound effects, and graphics. The video might only be for an audience of one, but that person will be a part of Frank's extended family, so I want to do my best.

An hour and a half later, we're laughing at the finished piece as Mom comes in, wearing her scrubs. At first she's surprised to see new footage of Frank, but as she watches, she breaks into a huge smile. When it ends, I'm shocked to see her eyes are misty.

misty

"I'm going to miss him too," she says. "Very much."

We spend our last weekend with Frank taking turns holding him, watching TV, and giving him his favorite snacks. Bodi continues to sense something's going on because he follows Frank from room to room like a shadow.

Matt and Carly stop over to say goodbye. Carly tells us all about the taping and that the show will air on Monday. None of us can believe she and Umberto got to meet Hugh Jackman in the green room!

Because the show is on at three—the same time as Mr. Ennis's class—he said our last class can be a viewing party. My mom's so happy for Carly that she reschedules a meeting so she can watch the show when it airs.

reschedules

With multiple visits from Carly, Matt, and Umberto, it's a busy weekend. When I put Frank in his crate Sunday night, he heads straight for his blanket to fall asleep.

From his first day with us, I knew Frank would have to leave someday. We were a foster family, a place to live with people before beginning his real work to help someone with disabilities. This day was always coming—I just hoped to put it off as long as possible.

"Good night, buddy," I tell him. "The pleasure's been all mine."

# FAREWELL

Mary shows up like clockwork first thing Monday morning. Mom said I could go to school late so I can say goodbye to Frank, but I think it's because she wants me to apologize to the director in person.

I hear them talking about Mary's flight as I walk toward the kitchen with Frank to hand him over—the same kitchen where I first met Frank two years ago.

clockwork

The woman who brought Frank here then was an older woman who seemed like a grandmother. The next person from the foundation who came was named Wendie. She visited us after Frank had an "incident" with swallowing one of my action figures and getting semi-kidnapped by Swifty who used to go to my school.

This new director looks different than I expected. Her hair is short, shaved on one side with bangs falling across her face. Frank must remember her, though, because he leaps out of my arms and into hers.

"Why, hello there, Frank." She holds back, waiting to see if he's comfortable with her, but he nuzzles her face like he just saw her yesterday.

She takes a step toward me and

nuzzles

holds out her hand. "You must be Derek. I'm Mary."

Her hand barely has time to touch mine before I blurt out another apology.

She listens to everything I have to say before she answers.

"You know what we call that at monkey college?" she asks. "A teachable moment."

"That's what we call them here too," Mom says.

Mary looks me straight in the eye. "The point wasn't that you were pretending to feed Frank hot sauce, the point is that you had him on a treadmill, loose in the yard, and you were using him for your own gain. You know posting videos of your friends without their permission isn't cool, right, Derek?"

I now feel even worse than I did

when my parents first caught me. Whether it's because Mary runs the foundation, or that her voice is so calm, I really take in everything she has to say.

"It's not like Frank could sign a release form," I offer. "And he DID have fun."

greyhound

"Like a greyhound has fun at the dog track?" Mary asks. "Or elephants at the zoo—THAT kind of fun?"

Her eye contact is so intense, I want to turn away but can't.

intense

"We humans are privileged to share the planet with these special creatures," Mary adds. "First and foremost, our job is to protect them."

I feel Mom gently come up behind me and put her hands on my shoulders. "Derek's done a good job doing that for two years," she says. "I don't want the YouTube incident to take away from the fact that he helped us make a safe and happy home for Frank."

From his seat at the table, Dad gives me a slight nod to let me know he agrees. Knowing my parents are on my side—even through all my stupid mistakes—feels like the most important thing in the world right now. Bigger than my birthday and Christmas combined.

"Our capuchins make a lot of mistakes also," Mary continues. "We expect them to. The question is, do they LEARN from their mistakes? I've seen capuchins try to take the top off a water bottle hundreds of times," she says. "But if they really care about improving, they'll keep trying."

I could make a crack about how she's comparing me to a monkey, but even I know that would take the conversation down the wrong road.

"I made this video for whoever ends up with Frank." I hand her the DVD that Dad had to show me how to burn since I mostly use digital files. "It's full of instructions so Frank is properly taken care of wherever he goes next."

digital

Mary smiles. "I'm sure this will be very helpful. Thanks, Derek."

She spends the next few minutes signing paperwork with Mom.

paperwork

As Mary heads to the door, I ask if I can hold Frank once more before they go.

enormity

I press my forehead against Frank's and smell his monkey smell for the last time. The enormity of my loss suddenly bowls me over with sadness.

Mary must notice that I'm about to fall apart because she gently takes Frank and says a quick good-bye. As soon as she's out the door, I do something I haven't done in years. I'd call it crying, but the sounds coming out of me now are more like a wounded animal wailing than a kid sniffling through tears.

wailing

sniffling

"It's okay, buddy," Dad says. "Sometimes a good cry is the best thing."

I've got Mom hugging me on one side, Dad on the other, and Bodi on his hind legs, trying to reach me from the floor. Everybody's being kind. Everybody's being supportive.

It's just that everybody no longer includes Frank.

# YOU WANT ME
# TO WHAT?

After washing my face and spending some time with Bodi, Dad drives me to school. It turns out I only missed my first two classes. All that emotion this morning wore me out and I keep to myself for the rest of the day.

All everyone else can talk about is Carly and Umberto's appearance on *Ellen*. Half the people jammed

jammed

into Mr. Ennis's classroom at three o'clock aren't even in our class; they just want to see the show. Ms. McCoddle bought giant bags of candy from Costco, which she passes around in large bowls. I try to rally with my classmates but two things haunt me. First, losing Frank. And second, the conversation I need to have with Mr. Ennis after class. He's not going to be happy with how I sidestepped his rules and regulations in my YouTube channel. Not. Looking. Forward.

haunt

sidestepped

Mr. Ennis's hair is almost crew cut length as he films the proceedings with his GoPro. "This is really something," he tells Carly and Umberto. "Those of us who vlog for a living would KILL for an opportunity like this."

crew cut

Matt is throwing M&M's into the air and catching them in his mouth. Umberto's popping wheelies until he runs over Natalie's foot. Carly looks almost embarrassed by all the attention.

It's been a fun class—I learned a lot—but there's no shaking that feeling of loss too. If fighting with Carly made me feel like wearing a shirt that didn't fit, betraying my parents and Mr. Ennis and then losing Frank feels like a hole in the bottom of my gut. People say time makes everything better; I don't know if that applies to monkeys but I hope it does because this feeling of sadness and guilt really hurts.

"IT'S ON! IT'S ON!" Ms. McCoddle takes a seat next to Carly and squeezes her arm.

When Ellen dances, most of us jump up and down. The first guest is Hugh Jackman, who talks about his new blockbuster. During the commercial, everyone yells over each other, full of excitement.

The segment on YouTube kid stars is next and we all scream when Carly and Umberto come onstage.

"You're wearing a bow tie!" Matt yells to Umberto.

bow tie

"I went old-school," Umberto replies.

Ellen asks Carly what it's like to have such rabid fans. Carly answers confidently; she doesn't seem nervous at all. I'm guessing the girl jumping up and down in the first row is Power73, and sure enough, Carly tells us it is.

The audience loves Umberto's

clips too, as well as JR's, a kid from San Francisco who plays with his toys on-screen. He's been doing this for years and has three hundred million views.

Three hundred million!

When the segment is over, we all go nuts. Mr. Ennis holds up his phone. "Both Carly's and Umberto's channels are racking up colossal numbers," he says. "This week is going to be huge for you guys—NOT that that's the most important thing!"

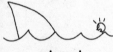
colossal

After Ms. McCoddle and the kids who aren't in our class finally leave, Mr. Ennis does a wrap-up of our work. Unfortunately, because my channel is no longer up, I come in pretty much last in every category. Luckily this elective isn't being graded.

"You guys have been great," Mr. Ennis says. "See you in the cybersphere."

I hang back while everyone else leaves, then approach Mr. Ennis.

"What happened to your YouTube channel?" he asks. "I didn't see it when I did a final pass of everyone's work this morning."

I begin to tell him the whole story of Monkey Love Hot Sauce.

He reaches up to shut off his GoPro. "But your parents signed the release forms giving you permission to upload that channel."

"I forged their name on the permission slip," I confess. "I did a fake show for them—they just found out about Monkey Love Hot Sauce last week."

Mr. Ennis lets out a low whistle.

cybersphere

KYLE
KYLE
forged

239 ★

harsh

"So you lied to me AND your parents? That is harsh."

"I knew it was wrong but I did it anyway," I admit. "Like those people you warned us about, doing anything for more views."

"One of my friends has a competitive-eating channel," Mr. Ennis says. "You don't want to know how many times he's gotten his stomach pumped chasing after views. Finding that fine line of connecting with people without chasing your own tail is what this is all about."

prickly

He pulls the GoPro off his head and rubs his prickly scalp. "I have to say, Derek, I'm really disappointed."

"Join the club—it's growing faster by the day."

Mr. Ennis smiles. "When I was your age, there was no mistake I

DIDN'T make. If there were a hundred things to choose from and ninety-nine of them were good, I'd make that one wrong decision every time."

"That's pretty much how I am," I say.

"That's why I'm a big believer in second chances."

He shows me the latest video on his phone. "I was approached by a major sports drink company to make a series of YouTube videos. They want me to do my illusions but to bring in someone younger to appeal to their preteen market."

approached

preteen

Go on. . . .

"I'm headed to Dodger Stadium this Saturday. I need a kid to toss fruits to me so I can swing at them with a bat and make it look like I'm

pitching

smithereens

turning them into the different fla-
vors of the sports drink. I was going
to ask one of my friends' kids, but
how's YOUR pitching arm?"

My mind flashes forward to me
on the pitcher's mound with a GoPro
on my head, winding up a kiwi for
Mr. Ennis to blast to smithereens.
This could be gigantic! A national
commercial! I take a breath and
try—for once—not to get carried
away. If Mr. Ennis is generous enough
to give me a second chance, priority
number one is to do a good job.

I tell Mr. Ennis I'd love to meet
him at Dodger Stadium. "If my parents will let me," I add. "I think I
might be grounded for a while."

"I just want to help you get
back on the horse," Mr. Ennis says.
"It would be a shame to give up on

being creative just because you messed up. You did some good work in this class."

The tension in my chest releases a tiny bit. Maybe I can resurrect my YouTube channel into something good that I DON'T have to lie about this time.

releases

resurrect

After all, when it comes to You-Tube, the possibilities are endless.

# THE COMFORT
# OF FRIENDS

Matt must be worried that I'll be lonely without Frank because he insists on coming over even though it's a school night. First we do our homework together, which we haven't done in years. Then we take Bodi to the park and throw him his chewed-up, soggy tennis ball until he collapses on the grass exhausted.

collapses

One of the things I love about

Matt is that he never worries about looking stupid or immature; he just wants to have fun. So when the toddlers at the playground get off the slide, Matt and I take turns sliding until a mom we don't know finally tells us to move on and give the little kids a chance.

Back at my house, Mom asks if we want something to eat.

"This may sound crazy," Matt begins. "But I would LOVE a smoothie."

"Sure," Mom says. "Strawberry and banana? Chocolate and peanut butter?"

My mouth is watering just at the MENTION of Mom's famous chocolate-peanut-butter smoothie but before I can answer, Matt suggests something else.

grimaces

"I was thinking more along the lines of an apple-juice-maple-syrup-clam-chowder-bagel-lettuce-and-blue-cheese smoothie," Matt says.

Mom grimaces and throws up her hands. "You two are on your own."

I realize Matt's staying at my house to make up for Frank not being here. I also realize Matt is one of the best friends on the planet. And as much as I'd TOTALLY prefer a chocolate-peanut-butter smoothie, I pretend that our gut-busting, disgusting con-coction is exactly what I want too.

We take over the kitchen and start tossing things into the blender like two mad scientists. We have to press pulse instead of on because the container is so full.

pulse

My dad sees us and looks around the room for a camera. "Is this some kind of dare? Are you guys filming this?"

I shake my head and tell him that believe it or not, we're doing this just for us.

Matt pours the brown goop into two glasses. He holds out his glass to mine. "To Frank," Matt says.

We clink our glasses.

"To friends," I say.

"To best friends," he answers.

"I'll drink to that." My dad grabs the blender from the counter, holds the container to his lips, and takes a giant swig.

swig

He immediately spits it into the kitchen sink. "That's DISGUSTING!"

"I know," I answer. "It's the blue cheese."

"Or the clam chowder," Matt adds.

yakking

Whatever it is, Matt and I spend the rest of the night yakking at the kitchen table and finishing our horrible smoothie till it's gone.

Not a bad way to spend a Monday night. Not bad at all.

# Want to learn about all the books in the My Life series?

Just turn the page!

## My Life as a Book

Derek Fallon has trouble sitting
still and reading. But creating cartoons
of his vocabulary words comes easy.
If only life were as simple!

## My Life as a Stuntboy

Derek gets the opportunity of a lifetime—
to be a stuntboy in a major movie—
but he soon learns that it's not as
glamorous as he thought it would be.

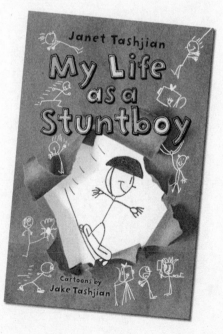

## My Life as a Cartoonist

There's a new kid at school who
loves drawing cartoons as much
as Derek does. What could be better?

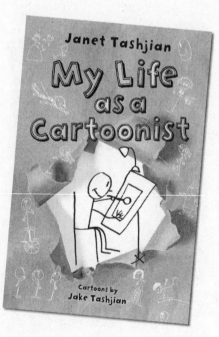

## My Life as a Joke

Now in middle school, Derek just wants to
feel grown-up—but his own life gets in the
way, and he feels more like a baby than ever.

## My Life as a Gamer

Derek Fallon thinks he's found his calling when he's hired to test software for a new video game. But this dream job isn't all it's cracked up to be!

## My Life as a Ninja

Derek and his friends are eager to learn more about ninja culture. When someone starts vandalizing their school, these ninjas in training set out to crack the case!

## About the Author

Janet Tashjian is the author of many bestselling and award-winning books, including the My Life series, the Einstein the Class Hamster series, the Marty Frye series, and the Sticker Girl series. Other books include *The Gospel According to Larry*, *Vote for Larry*, and *Larry and the Meaning of Life* as well as *Fault Line*, *For What It's Worth*, *Multiple Choice*, and *Tru Confessions*. She lives in Los Angeles, California.
janettashjian.com
mylifeasabook.com

author

## About the Illustrator

Jake Tashjian is the illustrator of *My Life as a Book*, *My Life as a Stuntboy*, *My Life as a Cartoonist*, *My Life as a Joke*, *My Life as a Gamer*, *My Life as a Ninja*, *Einstein the Class Hamster*, *Einstein the Class Hamster and the Very Real Game Show*, and *Einstein the Class Hamster Saves the Library*. He has been drawing pictures of his vocabulary words on index cards since he was a kid and now has a stack taller than a house. When he's not drawing, he loves to surf, read comic books, and watch movies.

illustrator